Stoop City

Stoop City

Kristyn
Dunnion

STORIES

A John Metcalf book

BIBLIOASIS
WINDSOR, ONTARIO

FIRST EDITION

Library and Archives Canada Cataloguing in Publication

Title: Stoop city / Kristyn Dunnion.
Names: Dunnion, Kristyn, 1969– author.
Description: Short stories.
Identifiers: Canadiana (print) 20200231316 | Canadiana (ebook) 20200231340
ISBN 9781771963862 (softcover) | ISBN 9781771963879 (ebook)
Classification: LCC PS8557.U552 S76 2020 | DDC C813/.6—dc23

Edited by John Metcalf
Copy-edited by Emily Donaldson
Cover illustration by Sybil Lamb
Text design by Gordon Robertson

Canada Council for the Arts | Conseil des Arts du Canada
ONTARIO CREATES | ONTARIO CRÉATIF
Canada
ONTARIO ARTS COUNCIL
CONSEIL DES ARTS DE L'ONTARIO
an Ontario government agency
un organisme du gouvernement de l'Ontario

Published with the generous assistance of the Canada Council for the Arts, which last year invested $153 million to bring the arts to Canadians throughout the country, and the financial support of the Government of Canada. Biblioasis also acknowledges the support of the Ontario Arts Council (OAC), an agency of the Government of Ontario, which last year funded 1,709 individual artists and 1,078 organizations in 204 communities across Ontario, for a total of $52.1 million, and the contribution of the Government of Ontario through the Ontario Book Publishing Tax Credit and Ontario Creates.

PRINTED AND BOUND IN CANADA

“Stoop, stoop; for thou dost fear
The nettle’s wrathful spear,
So slight
Art thou of might!”
(Francis Thompson, 1897)

Contents

Now Is the Time to Light Fires

IT'S LIKE LAST WINTER when she took that girl Lena on a road trip and left me to finish my thesis in the sub-zero gloom. Marzana is gone but her chattels prevail and everything, even the weeping fig she lugged from Ikea, evokes her. My Lorazepam shuffle wears a triangle from couch to bed to toilet back to couch, where I curl in her threadbare sweater.

Sleepless, dreamless, I up my dose.

The department offers bereavement leave and contracts my replacement, a kindness that permits me to stay home, forever pantless. I stack my research and drape it with cloth. Now who will argue the importance of historical processualism with archaeological data from pre-literate cultures? I draw the blinds. Stop changing, stop bathing. I eat cereal dry out of the box by the handful.

I'm not me anymore; I'm husk, shucked and forgotten.

After the truck hits, that's grief. Hydraulic pistons fire and the open-box bed lifts at its hinges: a dumping, a burial.

Nobody calls.

Nobody visits.

Every day is Sunday.

I light a candle. "You can come home now," I say to webbing that ghosts the empty corners of our room. I say to the drunkspun moths, "Come home!"

One day she does.

Marzana's lingerie drawer slides open and her garter dangles like a question mark. My spine zings with apprehension. Her perfume spritzes, infusing the room with her scent. The bed sheet turns down on her side.

I whisper, "Is that you?"

There's an indentation on pillow and mattress, a definite presence.

"You're here," I say.

She shimmers when I kick off bunched socks, toss my T-shirt, join her on the bed. I trail fingertips down my throat, collarbones, my scarred solar plexus. I falter—shy at last.

She hurled herself at me the night we met, a hastily bought rose between her teeth. I relive our drunken tango at last call, the halting, zigzag lurch back to my old place, necking against darkened storefronts, groping under clothes. Now, lying in our dusty bed, my hand works alone, intent and sorrowful, but a censoring pall hovers. Perhaps in her transformed state—nebulous, ethereal—she feels sexually inadequate? What allure does the primal realm hold for her now? I rest sheepish palms above the comforter and, suckling close, she spoons me instead. It's not warm flesh, but it's something. Old soup comes to mind, some kind of gelatinous substance, and I can hardly breathe for fear of crushing her in the night. Like she's a newborn or a kitten and not the crystalline essence of herself—her Soul infused with her distinctly flawed personality—that has transcended time and space, travelled countless unknown dimensions, returning against all odds.

All summer long we bump around the condo, relearning how to share this space. Nights, she settles against me and

I contemplate an eternity of abstention. Sex with Marzana used to be like shouldering an oversize grain bag, pouring, pouring an endless pile. The thinning rush over time, a lessening stream, the pitter and pat to empty. In her After Life she prefers not-quite-sisterly camaraderie—cuddling, hugging, holding hands.

I am pent. I simmer. But at least I'm not alone.

Marzana still roots through dresser drawers and abandons chucked clothing in piles on the floor. She stacks DVDs in towers by order of preference, her massive rom-com collection mocking me with sunny Hollywood covers. I survey her mess, mark a Cartesian coordinate system grid to impose order, and begin to excavate her cultural materials. I cradle and brush each item, starting in the southwest corner. I tag and label, jot notes.

This becomes my Stonehenge, my very own Pompeii.

Artefact 1.1: tucked in an overdue library book, I discover a black-and-white photo of Marzana at Hanlan's Point, a nudist beach I refuse to visit on principle. *Who took this portrait?* Marzana turned just as the shutter opened and her hair caught the wind, obliterating most of her face. But her mouth is open. Sensual, teasing. The lines of her body echo in the pines behind her, in the boardwalk strips and faded pier: she was disappearing even then, waving goodbye.

Other things surface. Things I do not especially wish to see. Phone numbers on tiny scraps of paper, some with lipstick imprints from hungry mouths. Love notes, an entire, incriminating series spanning more than a year from Lena, her so-called art-friend. Each piece of evidence spontaneously combusts in my hand or else Marzana ferries it out of reach. Those letters dance upon the ceiling, taunting. I string up clothesline and peg each charred, surviving remnant in chronological order, then cross-reference dates with my personal calendar.

An alleged out-of-town softball tournament occurred the same weekend as a particularly amorous getaway, recounted in gory detail by Lena.

Liars!

Marzana skulks behind her green recliner and, righteous, I fume for days.

It's bad enough she died. She had to cheat, too?

Marzana's mother calls. I stare at the phone but don't pick up and naturally she refuses to leave a message. Marzana retaliates by not coming to bed, which is fine because, frankly, I prefer to starfish the mattress, face planted, and I sleep better than I have since before it happened.

Artefact 4.6: a card from her family filled with their slanted, foreign cursive—squiggles and so many consonants. *Jare Święto*. It depicts old-world children parading from a small village to the river, carrying ghoulish dollies that they beat with sticks and set alight. Another incomprehensible springtime ritual that bears examination. An uncashed cheque floats out when I open the card. Marzana snatches it mid-air. I wonder, can we still deposit it? Nobody's haunting the electricity bill.

Soon the place is a booby-trapped eyesore. Dishes pile by the sink. Spills congeal in the fridge. Milk sours. A meagre harvest comes and goes. October bequeaths a snowstorm that eats November and I become almost as much a ghost as Marzana, padding barefoot on the frigid floor, confounded. If I could only assemble the clues correctly, I'd finally know: *who was she, really? What has she become?*

Our bickering escalates to dorm-room levels. Someone removes grid notes from the excavated artefacts; I find them taped to a box of maxi pads in the bathroom cupboard.

Someone dims the lights while I work, causing eyestrain and mental fragility. She feigns ignorance but I catch her twinkling with mirth. I crank the Gregorian chants she hates and my stereo disintegrates completely, leaving a blank square on the dusty shelf. Instead, her favourite song by that shitty Canadian band blasts the air, sourceless. Marzana's peace offering—finger-painted hearts boasting our initials—dribble condensation in the frosted windowpanes. I wipe them with an angry palm.

Caroline, department administrative assistant, says she has to meet with me. "Paperwork, you know?" She offers to do this off-campus. "It must be so hard," she purrs in the Tim Horton's. The release agreement sits before me, its tiny font devouring the page like so many ants.

"They're firing me?"

"You don't have to sign now." *Sotto voce*, she adds, "You might want to consult a lawyer."

Caroline smells sympathetic, like lilies, like gardenia. Her face is impossible: pink cheeks, lavender eyelids, perfectly groomed brows. Her skin is soft and powdered. I consider stabbing it with the plastic stir-stick.

"Marzana eats all the groceries, she won't do dishes. I can't even re-decorate," I confide.

She pats my arm. "I know you miss her, sweetheart."

Caroline's pretty face is a curtain, drawn.

"You think I'm making this up?"

Mortified, I abandon my green tea.

"Don't you want your donut?" she calls after me.

My throat sticks when I imagine opening the front door to our suite, breathing in that musty bog. *Terminated.* How will we live without my disability pittance?

Outside, I pace in front of our building. Snowflakes nip my face. They convene on my hair, my clothes. I have sneakers, not boots, and my feet slide on black ice hidden by the heron-coloured silt. Winter is coma-quiet and, just like Marzana's life, full of virulent secrets.

It may never end, this bone-clacking cold.

Wind rakes my flesh, pulls my nerves taut. It wakens something in my reptile brain, the part guarding ancient history, and I remember things weren't always terrific. This profound loneliness, this disappointment, had arrived long before she died. All those stay-home Saturday nights—too much dinner, bloated on the couch watching some anaesthetizing bullshit from her dread movie collection. But mostly, mostly, it was just me waiting for her to call or to finally come home: hammered, incoherent, and utterly blameless. She'd simply pass out, shoes still tied, forearms X'd on her chest, shut up like a pharaoh's tomb, mysteries sealed intact.

At the bar Pauly orders a double whisky and beer chaser for both of us. "Let me get this gay—your dead girlfriend is trying to get back together with you?"

"Yes. Well, I'm not sure."

"Like the dead husband film with Demi Moore. Ghoster's got balls," he says.

"Please don't call her that. Thing is, for the last year or more we weren't very sexual. Unfortunately, *that* hasn't changed."

"What are you telling me!" sings Pauly, ears covered.

"I can't even remember the last time I got laid. Okay, she's technically dead, but still. I can't take it anymore!"

Pauly says, "Drink."

I sip.

"Drink, now."

I drain my glass, set it down, wipe my mouth with a spaghetti-sauce-stained sleeve.

He says, "One, Ghoster was a jerk. Two, she cheated all over town and everyone knows it. Three, you need to shower and fix your hair and do something with your wardrobe. This is unacceptable."

In the mirror lining the bar back is an unrecognizable slob. A Dollar Store pom-pommed toque perches on greasy hair and Marzana's puffy orange ski vest draws the eye from my flannel pyjamas.

"What is this, some retro crystal-meth look?" He waggles his finger at my outfit.

"What was number two?"

"She was minge-munching with Lena in art history and all those gender studies babes. Leaving you home alone, wondering if your poon was gonna dry out. Girl up and dies and *now* she wants to hang? That's some serious cock-blocking."

"You knew about this?"

"Best not to think about it."

"Why didn't you tell me?"

"You had your thesis. It would've broke you."

"Who else knows?"

"*Everybody.*"

"Bartender," I yell.

"Him, too."

"Another round!"

Pauly says, "Pick up someone hot. Do it in every single room. Put some bodies between you. Please shower first."

I lift my cup and stare at that last amber drop. Glass tilted, the liquor speeds toward me, spreading thinner as it reaches the lip. There is silence, and our new drinks arrive.

That night Marzana sabotages the dig site, chucking all our labelled discoveries around the living room. I sit wild-eyed in bed, recalling countless late nights and the times she never came home. Her preposterous excuses: the bus detoured, a poker game broke out, she fell asleep at the bar. I'd beg her to call. "At least I'd know you're safe."

"This insecurity is pathologically patriarchal," she'd say. "You should get some help. You're too uptight."

And yet. The private funeral at a church in the suburbs with her accusing family, little dog and all, included a dozen Polish relatives I'd never met. Tables sagged with the weight of their food. I recognized dishes from the carefully wrapped Christmas leftovers she shared when she returned each year, sated, pants open at the fly, rubbing her belly. Now, finally, I was invited. Magenta barszcz and uszka, boiled pierogi with sauerkraut and cream, herb-marinated mushrooms and the thick, salted-radish salad. I bit into a very sour pickle and could not swallow.

Marzana's family wept exuberantly. They spoke at once, so many sounds I had no ear for—the buzzing and shushing of angry babies. "Lesbijka," spat her red-eyed mother, and I knew this was somehow *my* fault, what happened, what she *was*. I had not been vigilant. I was worse than the Communists they'd fled. There was no way in, not one spongy breadcrumb to track inside the ancient, sunless forest of their grief.

In the morning an oversized bouquet in cut glass appears on the kitchen counter. *Forgive me*, the card says in her handwriting, and melts between my fingers, leaving an icy puddle. The vase holds mosses, tiny white and gold star-shaped flowers, the crumbled bark of emperor and tsar oaks, their dust over five hundred years old. Ferns uncurl, releasing the scent of Europe's last remaining primeval forest floor. We trekked that savage and holy parkland once. She declared her love enveloped by pine bramble, alder and spruce. Whispered promises amid the dropped dung of elk and tarpan, the almost-fabled wild Polish horses. Back in the utilitarian hostel we tried sharing first one then the other twin mattress, but could not bring ourselves to consummate those earlier sentiments. We uncorked a bottle instead.

"What?!" I yell at the vase.

A bison, one hairy-hided ton of nearly extinct European bison, emerges from the fern depths, knocking me flat as it materializes and fills the kitchen. Gargantuan. Its heat withers. The snorting, heaving immensity of it sends me foetal to the corner. Its massive, snow-caked hooves clack across laminate flooring before it leaps and vanishes through the locked sliding-glass balcony doors.

"No!"

I pounce on Marzana's twinkling mass in the green chair. Like falling into a swamp, the thick ooze of suspension slowing gravity. Mud slops heavily on my limbs, my torso sinks under its primordial weight as we wrestle onto the couch, off the couch, below the stinking sludge, across the living room floor, scattering her belongings in the muck. I am neck-deep, then up to my chin. I hand-over-hand climb the coffee table legs to keep myself afloat.

Mindy Day, couples therapist, ducks beneath the clothesline and picks her way through the living room dig-site disaster. "Well, first, I'm glad you finally followed up after, um, eighteen months. My notes indicate your partner did not attend the session." Mindy positions a Kleenex box in the centre of the splattered coffee table and perches on the cleanest, driest part of the couch. I'm relegated to the green chair. Marzana, of course, is late. "I don't usually make house calls but I acknowledge this is, uh, a unique relationship context."

Mindy pushes her glasses up her nose. "I'd like to remind you of my commitment to anti-oppressive practice and I think in this situation we, um, need to address the complex marginalization of the pre-deceased."

I say, "Is this a joke?"

Mindy shouts at the ceiling. "Can you hear me?!"

"She's dead, not deaf. Anyways, she's not here, for once."

Mindy frowns. "I'd like to open the floor for—what's your girlfriend's name?"

"We're calling her Ghoster."

"Um, that's not okay."

A shaft of light blasts the television. It turns itself on. The nauseating final scene of a film starring Tom Hanks and Meg Ryan. Marzana's secret shame: she'd watch, weeping in this very chair, and could not be consoled.

"This is her doing?"

"Who else?" I say.

Mindy reaches for a tissue, sniffling. "Clearly we have a lot of sadness here and lost romantic possibility."

"Or a con artist," I mutter.

Mindy says, "Loss. That's what *I'm* hearing. What are *you* hearing?"

Dust motes in a tinkling burst, like a fairy's motorcycle backfiring.

I say, "It's been almost a year. Why come back? She obviously didn't want me anymore."

Marzana shrinks into herself. She's a glowing light, dense and coiled.

"Hmm, anniversaries are potent. On the phone you mentioned a sex problem? We can never know all the contributing factors to a compromised sexuality," says Mindy.

"I thought hormonal imbalance or childhood trauma. I didn't want to make her feel bad."

"You know, it's not uncommon for couples or individuals to get a second wind," says Mindy.

"Her second wind was with everyone *else* she knew."

Marzana buzzes nearby, like bees swarming. It's not exactly menacing but I clutch a throw-pillow shield.

"I think it's important to hear from both parties," says Mindy, and Marzana retreats closer to her.

"She wouldn't talk then and she can't now. I want her to leave. I need to get on with my life."

"This is her home, too," says Mindy.

"I can't make the mortgage payments. This will be nobody's home soon."

"I'm feeling a lot of hostility. It's important to take responsibility for our anger and be judicious in the ways in which we express it," says Mindy.

"What are you saying?"

"It's possible to victimize others when we articulate our own pain."

My hands grip the green, thinning fabric. To recline, you have to wrench the lever and heave your weight—which she used to do joyfully. I force it back and the foot support bumps up under my legs. Above: the ceiling is a seagull's underside, cream with grey shadows, soft but unnerving. Tom Hanks pronounces his love for Meg Ryan. She laughs and cries. They embrace.

All lies. These are just stories we tell ourselves to forget what we really are.

"Fear is primal, it can paralyze," says Mindy.

"No shit."

Months ago, I waited for her parents at the hospital. I held her compact, peasant's body, her sturdy, stubborn bones, that remarkably poreless skin. Her round head, so full of brains but not one ounce of that other kind of knowing. Square hands, short fingers, the feathering white tendrils at the back of her neck. I remember shock, like a face punch. And fear—watering mouthfuls of it.

The living room haze thickens.

Marzana huddles on the couch beside Mindy, who drops her clipboard. "Is this—I feel something—oh my God."

"That's her."

I am so tired.

"This is very unusual," says Mindy. "May I hug you?" she over-enunciates. Her thin arms encircle Marzana's sparkling mass.

Who was I? The rent-paying stooge? If wife, then cuckold. A sometimes mother, never by choice. Not so much partner as family: steadying, buoying. Obligatory and, by its very nature, constricting. Harder to leave than a beloved chair.

An unbidden image of her beneath a disco ball the night we met. In truth, I yearned for seduction, a beguiling. And she delivered it, hunched in her leather jacket, beers double-fisted, crooning into my spellbound face. Much later I glimpsed a figment of that once-tender child, the trapped past she privately defined herself against: alone, mute, outcast in her new Canadian home, far from the refuge of her Babcia's embrace. That famished phantom child would not be sated, not even by her fairy-tale dissection, carving at my sternum, gorging on the pumping organ within.

A bubble isolates in my chest. It rises, travels my throat, face, up through skull and scalp, dredging the blackened sludge from my dowager lungs. It passes through skin membrane, hair, and pops above my head, releasing me.

Clemency.

Mindy blows her nose beside Marzana's muted glow. Says, "To combat fear we must take action."

For once I agree. Now is the time to light fires, steal cars. To run and leap and fight and fuck and never lie down again.

I collapse the chair upright.

Mindy says, "I'm going to need help processing all this."

I say, "I'm going to need help cleaning this mess."

I write down an address in full. "Bring her tonight."

I pull on a sweater and dark wool coat from the closet. The wire hangers dance and clang, clang against their desolate neighbours. I lace boots, put on gloves. I don't say goodbye, just shut the front door when I go.

Pauly messages everyone, and they message everyone else, and the bar is overrun by midnight. It begins all stemmed wine glasses and buckets of hummus. Later, it's soggy embraces with shots of whisky, then hefts straight from the bottle. Full bottles replace empties. Out on the snow-dumped street we sing and march and hoist a makeshift dolly high on a stick. We shoot firecrackers, abandoned the weekend it happened. Mindy arrives with Marzana, a stupefied glimmer that caresses the scarfed and mittened crowd, thinning out so each person begins to sparkle a little.

I soak a rag in kerosene, tie it around the puppet. Pauly helps me light it.

A flicker, a flare: a white-gold whoosh with orange tongues and blue teeth, all the colours born of fire. We shout and cheer and dunk the smouldering pile into a pitcher of beer.

Ashes, they're everywhere.

"Let's go inside," says Pauly.

Bodies shed layer after layer of clothing. They gyrate on the dance floor. It's an episode of Girls Gone Wild, but morose: hair-tossing, nose-blowing mayhem. Mindy, stripped to her brassiere, dances erratically atop a large speaker.

"Did Marzana sleep with all these sobbing women?"

Pauly hands me another drink. "It's entirely possible."

He tamps pills out of a baggy. "You want?"

I open my mouth to say no and in they go, onto my tongue.

He ruffles my hair. "Let it flow, sister."

After the initial weirdness, after a glass of water and deep breathing in the corner, he leads me to the centre. He is a slim, dark river, twining and sucking. His exquisite movement renders me helpless. He twirls me around, around. Under the disco ball in the mirrored reflection beside him is a wolfhowling shadow.

Who is that sliding and stepping and shimmying with rage?

Who unleashed that unclean beast I swallowed as a child?

For hours, Pauly dances me outside myself under the neon lights that pulse in time with the beat. It's ritual, gay ritual. We mourn with sweat and style. We outlast the moon and all of the stars. We taxi home at dawn.

How We Learn to Lie

JULIA would have done him in a heartbeat, before. Tall, mid-thirties, good-looking in that manicured Ken-doll way. Today, in Docker shorts and flip-flops, symmetrical lightning-bolt tattoos revealed on his calves, the fantasy is ruined: just another aging jock-gone-wild. The client's cologne overpowers the tiny bathroom where his fiancée and Julia are trapped, Julia furthest in against the rusted-out tub, an amateur mistake for a realtor with her experience.

Tap tap tap. The client knocks his fist against the bathroom wall like he knows how to sound out struts. Probably saw that on television.

"Hmm." His fiancée frowns into the funhouse warp of a medicine cabinet mirror. When she copies him, rapping her knuckles against the stained wall, peels of paint fall into the sink like shells from a hard-boiled egg. She sucks on the pink straw jutting from her meal replacement, making it squeak. All elbows, knees, and clavicle—she's starving herself into a gown she'll wear one night only.

"What about that condo up the street?" says the fiancée.

Squeak.

"Nothing listed, but I'll keep you informed," Julia says. The hell Julia'd want them moving into *her* building. Sweat trickles Julia's hairline. Her blouse adheres to skin in the airless room. "There's another bungalow around the corner and a townhouse two streets over. I can get appointments for tomorrow."

"A buddy told me about the new build site on Dupont." The guy swoops closer and Julia has to crank her neck. He can hardly take his eyes off her legs in the new Louboutin heels.

"Towers are fifty percent pre-sold but suites won't be ready until late next year, if." Julia discretely dabs her temples and above her lip with a monogrammed hankie. She has to take them everywhere now, in case.

"Across from that junkyard?" The fiancée pushes past her man and wanders to the kitchen, opens the derelict refrigerator, wrinkles her nose, and shuts the door.

Julia wants out but the guy leans into the dusty doorframe, blocking her.

"This is a hot intersection. Prices will definitely skyrocket," says Julia.

"Got to think long term, babe," he says over his shoulder. "We could flip this bungalow and move into the condo in a couple of years. Make some cash-ola."

"I don't know. Daddy might not like that."

Squeak squeak.

The guy steps closer and Julia's face is inches from his button-down shirt, from the black chest hair curling against cotton. Undershirts, they're for a reason. Ten bucks says he texts later, after his fiancée is dosed on chardonnay and Ativan. She admires his confidence, but.

"Doesn't help for your wedding deadline," she says.

The skin beneath his eye twitches and he lurches into the hallway.

Julia gives them three years. Less, if they try to renovate this shithole.

"Is that mould on the ceiling?"

The fiancée stabs her straw into the drink container, churning the ice inside.

The least of their worries. If they'd bothered to google the address, they'd have read about its former incarnation as a crack den. They'd know about the human torso buried and unearthed in the yard, for example.

As an undergrad two-and-a-half decades ago, Julia never set foot in this neighbourhood. It hosted an alarmingly high arrest ratio for the city. Seven years back, when she pre-bought in the first building to go up, she had to steel her nerves. She drove everywhere, doors locked, pepper spray in her purse. Scummy strongholds, most notably the Coffee Time, continue to stage local drama. Fights—usually just yelling, but sometimes fists or geriatric kickboxing, sometimes a knife or two-by-four. And sex workers—streetwalkers, her mother used to call them—strut the donut shop parking lot with greased ponytails and short-shorts. Shrieks penetrate the floor-to-ceiling windows in Julia's concrete tower, and all night long men prowl the shadows like stray cats, pissing on everything.

"I'll wait outside while you have another walk through," she says. She wants to plan dinner with Jeff, who's not returning her texts. Plus she has to prep the young widow's condo for a weekend open house. Julia shields herself from the late August sun with massive Karl Lagerfelds and prepares for more heat.

Earlier that morning, applying collagen serum in her ensuite, Julia heard the dogs next door, *again*. She perched on the toilet seat and whistled into the vent to quiet them. Moisturized the corners of her eyes, the length of her neck, then her whole face, upward strokes only, before they started back up. Her forehead, smooth but beginning to tingle when she pressed, would soon need another treatment. She's got prepaid vials *on ice*, part of the introductory offer at the anti-aging clinic. While the cream absorbed, she stalked her tidy apartment, white and tan natural fabrics, glass with metal highlights. She cocked her head—more yapping.

"That's it, I'm saying something."

Jeff protested, then skulked behind.

In the fawn-coloured hallway, chrome-plated wall scones buzzed. Somewhere behind drywall, a toaster popped and silverware clattered on ceramics. Distantly, a shower was running. Julia rapped firmly on the door, and a fracas of high-pitched barking ensued. Four Boston terriers named after the Ramones.

"Joey's my favourite," said Jeff.

"You can tell them apart?"

She knocked again. "I know she's in there."

The dogs went berserk, piling against the door, claws scraping wood.

"Hmm," said Jeff. "You don't like little dogs, do you?"

"I'm emailing the board," said Julia.

"Maybe they don't like being alone?" he says.

"*They* can never be *alone*."

Back in Julia's apartment, Jeff spread his meticulous layer of peanut butter on dry toast. Julia scrubbed her cereal bowl, furious. "I can't think with all that noise."

"We could maybe help. Walk them when she's at work?"

"We?" Julia sucked in to zipper the Prada skirt and hook it shut. She checked her silhouette in the mirror. Fixed her blouse. Removed the Louboutins from the tissue paper in their pristine box, and stepped into them.

No way were those dogs coming in here. Hair everywhere, and you can never get rid of the smell.

The widow—they hadn't married, despite changes in same-sex legislation, so technically *not* a widow—is finally packing, but there's a lot to do before the open house. Julia will definitely earn her commission on the sale. Kitchen drawer contents have been dumped on counter and table, and the woman is muddling through, one piece at a time. "We won this Dolly Parton spatula at a dance party," she sniffles. A clothes bomb has gone off in the bedroom. The living room is a battlefield.

"I can drop a load at the Goodwill on my way home," Julia says.

The woman shrugs. "Her mother wants some of it."

"What about these posters, are they coming down?"

"I guess?"

A slew of bands Julia has never heard of: L7, Lunachicks, the Gossip. Lesbian music, she supposes. Julia checks her watch. She still has to pull stage props from her storage unit near Liberty Village before dinner downtown.

"Practicalities," Julia says, leaning against a bar stool. The shoes look fantastic but her feet are beginning to suffer; a blister is coming up on her large toe mound. "See if her parents will take that old armchair. It's got to go. Focus on packing your own things, plus the mementos you want to keep, and put them in the storage cage downstairs. I'll book a moving company to pack the rest. You'll get fifty thou more if we empty and power-clean the whole apartment."

The woman nods through tears.

Pity and something less charitable make Julia want to shout, *Burn it! Walk away with nothing. Find out who you really are!* Instead, she pats the woman's shoulder. "This is your chance to earn back from your investment and use it however you want. You can't get back *into* the market, not here, but you could do very well in a smaller city. Like, Windsor?"

Julia is just one woman giving tough love to another woman—the surface-level, getting-by-in-this-flawed-world advice, not the deep truths we quietly long for. Not unlike Julia's hard-nosed mother, now strapped into bed at the long-term-care home. Dementia suits her. Scottish and remote as the moon, she had unexpectedly handed Julia a cheque for one hundred and fifty dollars after her high school graduation ceremony, back in the day, *to help her get started.* Plus two weeks' eviction notice. She'd be renting Julia's bedroom for cash from then on.

Outside, humidity hits her full force, a hot wet garbage wind. Heat creeps her décolletage, up her throat, and the hair at the nape of her neck curls with sweat. Her blouse sticks to her spine, to the fine rivulet of perspiration running down it. The soon-to-be-married client has already texted: *drinks?* Julia's thumb hovers. She decides to ignore him. Still no word from Jeff, so Julia cancels their reservation. She needs to change her shoes, anyway. A cramp is starting in the arch of her right foot. She cranks the air conditioner in her Acura hybrid, and, after the cold air has blasted her to tranquillity, nudges the car into traffic.

Groceries, liquor store, the dry cleaner, then home. At the stoplight, she stares into a derelict lot destined for development. On the other side of the chain-linked fence an old woman stoops to pull weeds. One gnarled hand grips a woven basket, the other tucks the plants inside. Phase one of the project is soil remediation: months of delay thanks to some nosy environmentalists. Julia should warn her—toxins from the old paint factory. Julia lowers the passenger window, is blasted by the hot stench of gelatine-factory air, and the impossibly wrinkled face. "Med-i-cine," the woman says, nodding and smiling. Someone pushes a cart piled with empties along the sidewalk and Julia can't hear over the din, although the woman's mouth is still moving. It's unsettling—Julia is struck by an impulse to heed her advice, whatever it might be.

One, then two and more car horns lay into her; the light has turned green. Julia squeals through the intersection.

In the underground parking, Jeff's car is still in her spot.

"Shit," she says, and struggles with a seven-point turn, re-emerging to compete for street parking since the visitors' spaces are full. It's harder, now the towers have gone up. Julia juggles briefcase, shopping bag, and wine bottles the two blocks back to her building. She can't reach her door fob, zippered into her Gucci satchel.

Shit shit.

One bottle, the organic pinot noir, slips from its paper bag. She clamps onto it with her left elbow, that and the whole-grain baguette. The concierge, ever helpful, must be on break. She hears people in the lobby but can't wave and risk dropping the wine. She waits, body contorted and sweat-drenched, face reddening, while the amiable voices grow louder.

"It's so great they like you."

"I'm really comfortable around animals."

"That's, like, great."

The door pushes open and Julia exhales. "Thanks," she says. Jeff is with the wriggling, ecstatic Ramones and her neighbour, a petite woman in workout gear—tights and tank top. The woman's sculpted ass is taut and round. No wonder she refuses pants.

"Nice shoes. Do you live here?" she says to Julia.

"Obviously." They pass each other in the lobby and share the elevator every couple of weeks. Julia was the first to buy in with the developer, scoring the penthouse at an excellent price. She is already offering her briefcase from under one bent arm, but Jeff doesn't help.

"Oh hey, we're just going to walk them," he says. "See you upstairs?"

Julia jams her shoulder in the door before it shuts. Jeff and the woman take two leashes each. Boston terriers fill the sidewalk, a black-and-white military brigade. It's like an ad for online dating. Handsome man with greying temples and younger woman, so many white teeth. All those miniaturized pups, surrogates.

A hot lick shoots across one breast, lodges under the tip of her ribs. It's a tightening, a sharpening, and Julia's mouth opens, wanting air. There's a hot coal in her throat. Sweat stands on her upper lip, runs her hairline, pools in her cleavage. A deluge overtakes her. She stumbles into the lobby, makes her way to the elevator, leans heavily on the button, kicks off the thousand-dollar shoes as the bags dribble out of her clutch, and she descends onto all fours, gasping on the carpet, raging. On nineteen she hoists the bags, the purse, clenches a heel in each fist, baguette between her teeth.

Julia dumps the groceries on the polished granite breakfast bar that separates the space-age kitchen from the living room's expanse. Sets the Louboutins, blood-stained from her blister, back in their box. Lays the bottles—golden chardonnay like butter, the pinot noir, a plumb abyss—in the cast-iron rack. She pours a glass of cold water, downs it, pours another. On the balcony she gulps humid air, thick as honey. The ends of her hair frizz.

Along the horizon obstructed by gleaming towers, she can almost glimpse the street her father grew up on. Off-the-boat Irish, his then-young parents rented a series of rickety homes alongside other immigrants: Christie to Bathurst, Bloor to Dupont; now the elite, exorbitantly priced Annex. Julia's grandfather made bricks over in the Don Valley: hard, repetitive labour. Her grandmother cleaned for a Rosedale family, worked a half-dozen menial jobs to keep them fed. If only they'd figured a way to buy back then, before anyone understood the increasing value of land, before they were run off to dumpier neighbourhoods and to the burgeoning suburbs. Julia'd spent years inching her way back downtown.

In the retirement wing connected to her mother's secure ward, her dad sickened to grey when Julia told him how much her condo cost.

"Highway robbery," he sputtered.

"Look."

The real estate flyer listed a house he'd lived in as a child, still for lease by the same owners. She thought the photos would cheer him up.

"Five grand a month, plus utilities," he hooted. "They probably bought the whole house for that price!"

"Dad, are you alright?"

"Back then, five grand was as impossible to save as a half million is now. My parents couldn't escape poverty, coming here. At least we didn't starve."

"What are you talking about?" said Julia.

"They didn't know they'd be stealing from other people, here," he muttered, gazing out the bird-shit-streaked window. "All so I could go to school. So you could buy your condo." He slumped into his chair, morose.

"Have you taken your pills today, Dad?"

Julia buzzed the nurse.

But suddenly she was remembering weekends her mother thrust them both out, demanding a few hours of peace. Her father would head into the city in the blue Plymouth, pointing out childhood haunts to ponytailed Julia: Christie Pits where he lost his front teeth in a ballgame, the Italian sub shop with his favourite meatball sandwich, and Margueretta, the toughest street in town (now festooned in rose bushes and a new wave of yummy mummies whose strollers cost more than her Dad's car). The cinema where he spent rainy-day dollars, now, to his horror, exclusively screening porn.

An ambulance siren cuts through the intersection below: brick, cement, asphalt. Anaemic trees held hostage in metal cages, battered and leafless. No sign of Jeff and Yoga Pants and those terrible little dogs. A busker croons *I walk the line* in front of the donut shop, tiny guitar amp on wheels, upturned hat collecting coins. The sky shifts: storm clouds in the northwest with faraway thunder.

Rain is coming. She can taste it.

Last winter was so mild that, on their second date, they took drinks out and leaned over this same balcony railing. Were two sips in before Jeff dropped to his knees, pushing up her skirt. He peeled down the elastic waistband of her pantyhose, yanked when they stalled at her hip, ripping the crotch. He was starved for sex, to her delight, and was a bit of an exhibitionist. After, she balled the shredded mess in her fist, lobbed it over the edge. Wondered briefly if it might land on Jeff's own balcony, a few floors below, for his wife to discover. Instead, the crumpled hose caught an air current that gusted down the stand of newly erected buildings, sheer legs flapping as though waving goodbye.

Inside, calmer now, Julia pours a blend, neat. Whisky warms her mouth, draws a finger of fire down her throat to her empty belly. Threatens to incite another hot flash. What a joke. She and Jeff managed to keep their fling under wraps for several weeks before his wife, a beige-wearing elementary school teacher, kicked him out. *Good for her*, Julia thought at the time. He'd brought his bags up to the penthouse, sheepish, promising to find his own place soon. That was almost six months ago. She swirls liquid gold in her glass.

She'd made it too easy.

Jeff was not her usual type. Less ambitious. Potentially kinder. A decent investment, or so she thought. She liked to palm his solar plexus, heart pumping under the meat and gristle and cotton-polyester of him: a solid, regular comfort.

Julia preheats the oven and pulls a box of veggie burgers from the freezer. Since Jeff, a long-time vegetarian, moved in, she's given up meat but sometimes all she craves is rare steak, bleeding into the bun, smothered in sautéed mushrooms. When the beeper goes, she slides in the pan. Tosses a green salad with hemp seeds, shreds carrots and beets. Crushed garlic, Dijon, apple cider vinegar, pomegranate molasses, and a stream of very nice olive oil gets whisked into the dressing: her ex-husband's recipe. The burgers are flipped, then ready.

Still no Jeff.

She turns off the oven but keeps them warm.

A half hour later, Julia smothers a dried-out patty in BBQ sauce alongside the wilted salad. Keys jingle in the lock and then he's in, eyes averted, dropping a distracted kiss on top of her head.

"Dinner's in the oven," she says evenly.

"Oh, I picked up a falafel."

Sweat, on her upper lip. Again.

Jeff hunches on the couch. Flicks on the hockey game and alternates staring at the large screen and thumbing through messages on his phone. Julia presses a kitchen towel to her face and neck, her cleavage. She pours a glass of wine, plugs the bottle with a sterling stopper.

"Open house this weekend. Working late. You?" Julia marks it on the healthy-living calendar that's taped to the fridge.

"Consults," he says. "Tuesday's an early one."

Julia rinses her plate and stacks it in the dishwasher. She could wrap the uneaten food for tomorrow, but swipes it into the bin instead. Next time he can make his own goddamned dinner. She tops up her wine glass, settles beside him on the couch, and switches her glass to the other hand so she can scratch the back of his neck.

He's rapid-texting, thumbs drumming the miniature keyboard.

"Who's that?"

"Hmm."

Julia takes the remote and shuts off the power. The living room expands in the absence of noise and the television's incessant flicker.

"Beer in the fridge," she says, propping sore feet on the ottoman. If her skirt weren't so tight, she'd be able to massage her instep. Julia drops her hand onto Jeff's thigh and he flinches. He gets up and opens the fridge, pulls out a beer, fumbles for a pint glass, and pours his bottle out slowly. During which time she scrolls through his phone history. She sets the phone down. Exhales.

"That thing loves misery," he's saying, and she has no idea what he's talking about. "Honestly, I'm sure she needs the company, but is it fair to the animal?"

"All's fair in love and war," says Julia.

She's already imagining what she will hang on the wall in place of his TV.

Jeff zaps the TV back on and sits heavily at the end of the couch. He hadn't arrived with much, other than clothes. Still has boxes in the ex-wife's storage. Wife, technically. Their divorce hasn't even gone through. On the screen, sticks slap ice. Bodies smash into boards painted with corporate logos. The whistle. *Time out.* Blood rushes her ears, pulse knocks her teeth, as she replays the text sequence over and over:

"that wuz hot"

"yr hot"

"c u @ yr place"

Emoji. Emoji. Emoji.

During that sustained limbo before her own divorce, Julia dated a series of men she met online. Professional, clean-cut, moneyed. She preferred dark hair, although she dabbled with one blond investment banker. Blonds seemed less smart. She liked them married, arrogant: men with an edge. Casual sex took them down a peg; she blew off steam but didn't upend her domestic routine.

Derek was unobtrusive, considerate: a good wife. Julia and he had married after university, where Derek had majored in law, she in business, like her father. She assumed Derek was happy the way things were, except for the fact they had no children. Memories pursued her—Derek lying naked, mouth pinched tight, her hand pumping his member into usefulness, and a clumsy straddling of his torso. She'd cup his softened genitals in one hand, fighting the impulse to crush him. Their sex was effort and embarrassment and very little release. But Derek remained hopeful, applauding Julia's careful multi-vitamin regime, never realizing she'd poured her birth control supply inside that other bottle. After sex, Julia would catch Derek sneaking potato chips from the top shelf of the cupboard. On tiptoe, his belly slopped over the waistband of his boxers, those rounded shoulders reminding her of an old aunt she hadn't seen in years. It disgusted and also endeared him to her, provoking fits of weeping in the bathroom, a hand towel pressed to her mouth.

Reclining in the living room, paperback tenting his lap, Derek absorbed her far-fetched explanations night after night. Julia visualized a freshly poured concrete wall, thick and impenetrable—a work trick she used during negotiations. It kept her immune to the insinuation in Derek's enquiries, his red-rimmed eyes.

Eventually she got caught.

She once met a trim financier from Newmarket on the beach where she stripped, flattered when he snapped a few photos, *for later*. At the hotel he got rough, pulling her hair, calling her names. *Slut*. The word turned things. She floated to the stained pressboard ceiling and watched the rest unfold, somewhat sickened, as she had often felt in her teenaged, pre-Derek dating years. After, the guy checked messages while sprawled across the germ-magnet polyester bedcover. A meeting back at the office, he said. He dressed quickly and did not make eye contact. How could she know he lied, that he was actually an insurance lawyer who worked downtown at none other than Derek's firm? That he routinely shared photos and gory details of his *fucked-up bitches* with guys at the office? Most shocking, that Derek participated in this sort of conversation? Julia was in no position to judge. She had severed whatever rope tethered them. It stung, naturally, but was enormously instructional.

She rented during the divorce settlement. Afterwards, with her share of the house proceeds, she put a down payment on the penthouse when it was still in the design phase. Shrugged off her mother's accusatory stare, her father's bewildered questions. They liked Derek, possibly more than they liked *her*. He was reassuring in all the ways Julia could never be, and friendlier. She lost Derek's friends in the bargain. But she got to choose her own cabinet colours, appliance upgrades, backsplash, and bathroom tile. It reminded her of the Barbie dream home she loved as a little girl. Her first exhilarating foray into real estate, and property values had already gone up forty-three percent. She bought another unit to rent out, has her eye on a third. Julia is growing capital, making money. This time she's not sharing it with anyone.

In the morning, Julia changes the locks with her power drill after Jeff leaves for work, and now his things are waiting by the door, packed. He'll have to make arrangements. She should never have let him stay in the first place. The trick is to be firm. She will not argue; as a kindness, really. Instead, she focuses on her open house. She's taking before-and-after shots for her portfolio. Her commission on a decent offer will pay two months' rent at her parents' care home, plus a Netherlands retreat, where advanced spa technology has incredibly youthful results.

Julia is going to look amazing.

The lesbian widow is staying with friends for the weekend. Did she even *try* to tidy up? Julia hires a cleaning service, and she and the maids go to town. She takes breaks to mop sweat from her hairline, lets wind from the balcony cool the hum of her hot rage when it surges. She texts Lightning Bolt, her other client, the jock fiancé; something noncommittal, obliquely encouraging. She wants to close the deal first. Meanwhile, the dead girl's family is sniffing around for money, making accusations. Julia wants zero interference until the papers are signed. "Prenups, they're not just for straight people," she'd said as kindly as possible.

After, when all is spotless, Julia angles the furniture, sets the lights *exactly*. No photos. Large mirrors in every room so potential buyers literally *see* themselves in the space. She brings props: DKNY shower curtains with matching bath mat and towels, a fluffy robe, all plush fabrics in neutral colours. A burnt-sienna shag rug provides the colour hit for the main space, which is filled out nicely by oversized palm fronds. A pot of yellow and orange mums out on the balcony draws the eye and attunes potential buyers to primal, subliminal associations: creamy butter and gold coins and the molten star at the heart of our solar system, the source of all life as we know it, the sun.

The bedroom is tricky.

It must deliver comfort and security. Intimacy *and* anonymity. Evoke the possibility of adventure yet reassure monogamists. For couples, she needs to demonstrate connection *and* personal space, something she frequently attains by using miniaturized bedside tables with matching lamps, and by leaving a wide berth around the bed. The bed itself must be the focus: an appropriate skirt to cover the box spring, very high thread count sheets, and a stylish comforter that pulls the room together. All the emotion comes from the impeccably selected throw pillows.

Julia hums as she works. She pulls and tucks and folds the sheets, erasing the past: repetitive, careful gestures. As a teen, her first job was at the local motel. She learned to clean from an old German housekeeper. Smoothing linens with military precision is an unsung tradition in the janitorial arts. A properly made bed can console the itinerant, the brokenhearted, the homeless. Staging properties, she has learned over the years, is mostly about subtraction, about deleting personal history, something she takes very seriously. She continues to take things away with total exactitude, one after the other, until a purity in openness emerges, a balancing of light and air and material objects set in space; the lie of neutrality. This is the soothing of wounds, when complete; the calming of sorrows. Progress and satisfaction, here on earth.

Fits Ritual

"**I DUNNO, ROAM.** I don't feel so good."

I lean against a tree that's bursting obscene buds, hundreds of tiny pink cocks, part of the swish landscaping here in Yorkville. My head hurts, my face burns. I lick my lips and look over one shoulder, look over the other. Stick my head into the fancy fountain spray, the *rain curtain*. Open my mouth to those toxic drops.

"Gross," says Roam. He grabs my phone from my chest pocket and takes a bunch of kissy-face selfies.

"Yeah, well," I say, wiping with a dirty sleeve, shaking my hair.

Roam shoves my phone back into my pocket. "Come on, you promised."

"Ugh," I say.

Roam flattens one nostril. Snorts from a tiny bottle with the other, pitches it.

"It's on," he hisses, and I slink away.

Roam staggers. His eyes roll. His lips stretch wide, distorting the pretty symmetry of his face. Roam crashes to the cobblestone, startling the filmgoers, tourists in line at the festival box office. Tremors overtake him, his limbs thrash and wild sounds escape his drooling mouth.

"Get help," shouts an athletic blonde. She's the first to drop her shopping and run to Roam's spasmodic side, the first to lay her hands on his Hugo Boss button-down.

Gawkers drift toward them, and that's when I move, pick up the girl's abandoned shopping bags—Banana Republic and Chanel. I stuff the bags one inside the other, jam them into my backpack. Shoulder her Gucci purse with the gold-chain strap. I bump, then pull a man's billfold from his jacket, snatch a digital camera. Grab what I think is a wallet from a girl's bag, but it's a journal, a book of feelings, worth less than nothing, so I drop it. The crowd shifts, zooms in to the blonde. She's checking Roam's pulse. He's called off the shakes early. He's not even drooling. He whispers and strokes her cheek. She smiles, pinkening. They stare at each other with a wanting so plain it twists my stomach.

My focus wavers.

My mark, a middle-aged woman, looks directly at me.

Sees me.

"Thief!" the lady shouts.

Faces turn, hands pat pockets, mouths open wide, all slow mo.

"Thief!"

Kids erupt from the nearby alley, pushing for the subway entrance, oblivious.

I bolt. Blend with the herd. Headphones on, music cranked. "Gaytard! Loser!" they shout in each other's faces, like hyperactive morons, like regular kids our age. One whacks another with a school binder, laughing. We descend to the underworld, leaving Roam collapsed like a modern-day Christ, Mary Magdalene golden at his side.

On our bench at Moss Park, where we meet after the fits, I feel worse so I lie down to wait. If shit flies, like if he's scooped by paramedics and ends up in emerg, Roam calls and I bust him out. Today I wait and wait but there is no call, no text, no Roam. I pace from our bench to the twenty-four-hour convenience store back-up, Gucci shouldered, backpack heavy. Hang around till the clerk with the combed-out afro, puffed up like a storm cloud, tells me *beat it*. I shuffle back to the bench. Still no Roam. I can't shake the way he looked at that girl. The way he touched her face like it was holy, like it was a kitten.

My gut cramps. It's watery with a molten lump, hissing.

Roam is ripped. He's a mountain cat—a predator, perfect in his own skin, which I trace with fingertips, a tongue. Sometimes I wish his good looks would rub off, but mostly I'm just in awe. Everywhere we go, people want to get close to him and his fits give them the perfect chance. Roam could just zone out and blink for a couple minutes, and *still* get attention. But why be subtle? Roam loves to lose consciousness—it's more exciting that way. Roam can flop around for five whole minutes, which is good, since most folks need time to lose their inhibitions, to get involved. But if he goes on for much longer, someone will declare it a medical emergency and that is a total shitshow.

I stroll through the park past the safe injection site, admire the scraggly bushes, the patchy grass, sunshine.

Lies.

I'm freaking right out, shouting my mantra, "Roam throws the fits, I grab the loot!"

Where is he?

Back on our bench, I wipe sweat from my forehead, lick my lips.

My pains are ramping up.

After each crisis some Good Samaritan arranges Roam in the recovery position and blankets him with his very own tweed jacket. A halo of kneeling humans will then surround him, the fallen angel, and that's when he really shines. They overflow with decency, their own surprise at helping a beautiful stranger. Their goodness is an electric charge encircling Roam, his spotlight. No question: Roam is an honest to goodness star.

I'm invisible, another highly developed skill. I started training young—burrowing into the corduroy couch every time my mom opened a bottle. I'm completely forgettable: brown, brown, beige. Androgynous. Average height. Hair to the shoulder. Not skinny, not fat. I don't pay for the bus, they never ask. I'm a ghost—people pass through my life like I'm not even here.

Roam throws the fits; I grab the loot.

We bring in a decent haul, depending. Timing is everything. Rush hour's a joke. A person could die on a subway platform at rush hour and no one would look twice. Location is important, no use picking empty pockets. A rich intersection on a sunny afternoon, when tourists and yuppies are strolling around, thinking about the stuff they have and the stuff they want. They're thinking about what they're going to eat, who they're going to fuck, how they're going to spend their money. I don't blame them, I would too. They can afford to be curious—don't confuse it with humane. Sounds bad but it's true. If you saw a stud writhing on the ground, you'd mostly just wonder. And never underestimate the power of costumes. All you need is a dirty shirt or bad haircut and everyone assumes you're OD-ing, everyone's a judge. Paramedics are the worst, demanding tox screens and talking down at you. The first time Roam wore a Holt Renfrew shirt I stole off the rack, our take was triple. More than that, everyone tried to help. That's when the ritual took off.

"Of course," Roam said later, smacking himself in the head. "I could be their preppy son! Hoofy, why didn't we think of that sooner?" He smiled that treacherous wall of white.

Roam throws the fits. I grab the loot—iPhones, wallets, jewellery, watches. Bicycles. Hockey skates, once, and a freshly taped stick. It's a talent, what can I say? Everyone's got something. Sometimes, like today, people set down their shopping, receipts and all. Roam calls that a bonus round—random shit we return for cash, or take to Pawn City, or sell off cheap to guys at the shelter, guys on the street. Teddy Bears, lingerie, housewares. I could take or leave it, but Roam loves the rush of never knowing what we'll get.

"Like Christmas," he says, kissing me on the lips when it's over.

Roam is officially four hours late.

Usually I wait, part of the ritual, but I'm pissed, so I open the girl's purse. It burps cinnamon, and tiny gifts spill into my lap: tampons and chewing gum and crystal-studded barrettes. No cell. Must have had it in her jacket. A smooth leather billfold opens to plastic: no cash, but card after card and a driver's licence, and a set of keys that I jingle between my fingers. *Mackenzie Rutherford*. I tap her address into my phone and, what do you know, Rosedale. I sniff a lip-gloss applicator and apply sparkly goop, smack my lips once, twice. They feel better, prettier, and also slightly toxic.

Once, Roam got a mentor after the ritual, a businessman who believed in his potential. Harold Buchanan wanted to help Roam get *back on track* by going to college, maybe work his way up at Buchanan's medical billing company to pay off tuition. Harold recalled a time when he, too, had needed a father figure's guidance. Roam had no intention of working or going to college, so that plan fizzled, but I still have the man's card. Last summer an older woman, and I mean *older*, took Roam to dinner at a fancy restaurant with tablecloths and everything, with shit on the menu not even in English, shit no person should rightly be eating, like frogs and snails and birds with their heads still on—and then took him to her bed by way of *repaying* the gross dinner.

Roam has even scored girlfriends after the fits, something that never ceases to astound me. These girls crouch over him while he spazzes, like he's a baby bird dropped from a nest. They love his torment, love saving him. Think he'll be grateful and kind, since he's basically an invalid, a good-looking cripple, and probably not as big a jerk as most regular guys. Hah! They program their numbers into his phone after the seizure subsides, make him promise to call. Roam calls them Fitty Girls, and I can spot them right away, the real suckers. I make sure to lift their precious gift bags, their lambskin gloves, first.

"Ah, Hoofy, don't be jealous," he says, petting me. "They're not real, not like you."

But I do hate them, his suffering, helpful, rich girls. And not just that. I hate Roam when he's with them. When Roam hooks up with a Fitty, he disappears until he's bled their credit dry. Tells them pretty much the same story: he's twenty and three quarters, waiting for his next birthday so he can access an enormous trust fund. Sometimes he's the rebellious child of a tobacco tycoon. He expects to be kept at a very high standard, and mostly the girls are eager to please. They love investing cash in a hot boyfriend knowing that, in a few weeks' time, they'll be living even larger, just like the Kardashians.

Five hours late.

I pick my cuticles until they bleed. Check my phone—battery half charged, ringer on, zero messages. My stomach is a mess, growling. I open the man's wallet: eighty bucks.

Stuff the cash in my pocket. American Express, Visa, MasterCard—that's Roam's game. Ordering shit online, returning it for cash; selling the number and address, you name it.

The pain in my stomach shifts, heating a tight spot in the centre of my chest.

Screw Roam.

I dump the wallet with all those fancy credit cards into the garbage can beside the bench.

Later, I go back to the convenience store. Big-Hair Storm-Cloud growls at me, I swear, but I flash some cash and he lets up. I buy an energy drink: sugar and vitamins. A bag of chips: lunch.

Back to our bench.

The camera is a nice-looking Nikon, still charged. I take photos of the Sherbourne church and a pigeon, its walleye staring orange at me. I zoom in on my sneakers, my crotch. A shot of my face. Then I look through the digital roll. I am unrecognizable, even to myself. The pigeon is demonic. The Gothic church, foreboding. I keep swiping: kid on a swing, kid eating ice cream, kid chasing birds from a fountain. Hard to tell if it's a boy or a girl. There are dozens more, like TV commercials.

I delete every last one.

The hole inside grows—it's eating up a larger, darker space. The chest pain blooms. I tuck the camera away. My palms sweat. Forehead sizzles.

I need water.

Something.

Well, Roam, you are officially the biggest turd ever.

It's the time of day when the camera-family eats supper. Today I have cash, so I can, too. For a split second I'm an easy mark, daydreaming the places I could go, the food I could try, the people I might meet or become.

I go to Mickey D's, get a combo, the usual, swallow it down, regret it almost immediately. In the can I puke it all into a plugged toilet. Barf on my shirt, so I ball it up and pitch it in the garbage. There's a soft, white T-shirt in the girl's Banana Republic bag. *Ninety bucks*. Bite the tags off, slip it on. It fits great, deep V-neck so my titties almost show. The Chanel bag has a hooded jacket with zippers and pockets, little sparkling snaps. *Four hundred and fifty dollars*—total insanity, a whole month of welfare. But it's perfect for hiding the money. I trash the bags and receipts, the tags, my dirty clothes, but keep my backpack, keep the pretty purse on my arm. I fish out the barrettes and clip them in my hair, touch up my lip-gloss. I'm a runway runaway: sunken eyes, high cheekbones, concave torso. An old man opens the door and yells *get out of the men's room, you hussy!* I could show him my junk, but I don't have any fight left.

Back on our bench.

Teeth bang together. I'm shivering, can't fall asleep, but at least I look good. I'm groggy and hurting. Finally, finally, night comes.

I buzz the emergency-shelter intercom, dancing from one foot to the other.

"Is Roam here?"

A worker answers, Deandra, but her voice crackles with static.

"Hang on."

Eventually she trudges down and hauls open the door.

"Past curfew, Hoofy. Can't keep bending the rules, you know. Roam's not here. Coming in? Nice barrettes," Deandra says, ruffling my hair when I scoot past.

Inside, Carmell gets up in my grill. "Where's my money? Roam said today so cough it up."

"I don't got nothing, man, truth."

He says, "Oh yeah? Where'd you get the fancy clothes? Lah-dee-dah! Purse first, huh?" He strokes the chain strap up and down, moaning and gasping, pretending to shoot a load right on me.

"Relax, it's a knock-off," I lie, clamping my elbow tight.

Carmell knuckle-punches me on the arm, the arm, the shoulder, and once in the gut before Deandra breaks us up. "Settle it outside or tomorrow, got it?"

I hand Carmell the camera.

"You'll get coin," I say, and he goes, "Can I smoke this shit? Can I? Twat!"

"Hoofy, you don't look so good. Got the flu?" Deandra doses: two pumps of hand sanitizer. Says I shouldn't be here if I'm sick, that germs can spread cot to cot in the wide-open room. She pops a thermometer under my tongue and makes up a spare bed in the weirdo wing—for trans folk and the batshit crazy or both—for sickos like me. "Change your clothes and lock up that purse if you want to keep it, hon, you're on your own tonight."

I mumble, sweating and shivering at the same time.

My money. Don't take my money.

She says, "Fine, have it your way," tells me to get into bed. Her face stretches weird like a Muppet. Her eyes grow shiny and round. She calls the outreach nurse, but I crash hard in a dark world of twisting shapes and the relentless pound of marching boots, an army of bad guys herding me into a dead-end alley, shitkicking me in the dumpster, where I collapse, curl up, and die.

Two paramedics.

One is a total douche.

He says, "Last time this little shit stole the painkillers."

Deandra says, "I couldn't wake him up, God, I mean, he's really sick," and the ponytailed paramedic writes it all down.

Douchebag flips me onto the gurney, straps me in, purse and all, rolls me through the shelter, ramming into cots and hissing for guys to shuffle out of the way.

Carmell pops up with the Nikon and takes photos of me, of Douchebag, of Ponytail and Ponytail's ass. Click, click, click, click. "Hey! Wanna paaaaarty?" he says, swinging his hips.

"You wish," says Douchebag.

"I'm talking to the hot one," says Carmell. "See you later, Little Hoof."

In emerg, fluorescent lights blur, announcements scream over the PA, hospital staff squeak back and forth in their rubber-soled shoes. Chaos. A kid's got his arm stuck in a Pringles can. A drunk guy is bleeding from the head into his balled-up shirt, revealing the worst tattoo ever: a derelict Canadian flag across his hairy chest. An old guy paces back and forth, shaking a Tim Horton's cup and wheedling, "Spare change? Spare change?" The paramedics hacky-sack on either side of the gurney, with me face up in the middle. When it lands on my torso, they go, "Ohhh!" and Ponytail gets a point. Douchebag chugs an energy drink. A minute later, he says, "We're up. Shit, it's the Borg."

Her again.

They wheel me into a make-shift, curtained room, dump me with the crankpot nurse, the same one who tried to help me when I first landed in this city.

She says, "Hoofy, can you hear me? I'm checking your vitals."

So it begins.

Day after day she appears like a stain on the white cotton swathe, spreading her dark tools around me. The Borg takes piss, blood, all the pathetic details of my reject life, gives me big science in return. Puts me on a joyless regime once she figures out what I've got. There are other treatments, new ones, less horrible, but they cost. The biopsy is the worst. If you think your insides hurt, try letting some white-coated goon stab them with a needle. You'll know pain like a lover.

Pegasys—interferon, my horse with wings—and ribavirin, my endless pink pills. Every day I swallow them and then head to the park to crash on our bench like an old person, a squirrel-feeding pigeon-lover, until it's time for more pills. Nights, I fall asleep with my phone open to Roam's selfies, his close-up pouting lips. I take weekly needles in the thigh until they're too bruised, then in the gut. It's never easy. I still puke, and once I shat my pants, couldn't get to the can. The pain in my chest and my other friend, the belly cramp, become less like two warring neighbours, more like one neighbourhood gang in my torso. Like a sharp knife has slit me, crotch to the base of my throat. The day I imagine having to sell the gold-chained purse, barrettes long gone, I cry. Like a whiny-bitch-baby, I cry and cry and nobody comes, nobody has a Kleenex, snot streams down my face. *Roam throws the fits and he can fucking die, he can fucking die already*, and then I think shit, maybe he did, so I let her rip, sobbing and coughing till I'm finally all cried out, all the way down to a wimpy, snivelling sniff. Then I throw sticks at my favourite tree and kick the wide, barky trunk and swear my Roam-hate until a cop says *calm the fuck down kid or take a ride to 51 Division.*

Sitting, always sitting, this time at the clinic.

Brown paper bag from the Borg: peanut butter sandwich and two homemade cookies, which I nibble carefully. Really, Roam left me no choice. And I could use a break from this new life of mine, the strength-sapping hell of it, the endless misery. I open the stained purse, remove the billfold, slide fingertips across it like I do every day. What is it, seal foetus? Punch the girl's address into my phone for the millionth time. Pace the hall, round a corner. Peer into a room at an old old lady lying on a cot, bulgy eyes staring. Press a finger to my lips. Take hold of the patch on her arm, rip it right off her wrinkly skin. Her eyebrows round up and a strange sound whooshes out her mouth. Slap the pain patch onto my chest. *Better.* Quiet in the nurses' station. Scoop a crossword puzzle, sharp pencil, a partially eaten chocolate bar. Bite. Bite. Yum. Take the Borg's long wool sweater off the back of her chair, wrap it around my shoulders, tug the belt tight at my waist.

Outside, the Queen streetcar's back door beckons in the greying light. I ride for free. Take the bus up Sherbourne, belly roiling, hop off, puke chocolate into the road. Walk to Bloor. Down into the Don Valley, a wilderness. Bushes, brambles, long grass. Bees buzz. Hare leaps. Hawk overhead. The last star of night, a ghost moon sliver. Dog walkers; neon, crack-of-dawn joggers. Follow the GPS on my crap phone. Step in mud or maybe shit. Scrape it off with a stick. Head north forever, take endless stairs, rise up to another dimension with the morning sun: enter Rosedale.

Wide, quiet streets and no garbage.

Houses like mausoleums.

Perfect mowed grass everywhere.

Finally, map the red circle: I'm here. Stand on the manicured lawn, mansion set back from the road, marble statues, pillars, like some fucking TV show, the works.

Step and sniff.

Step and sniff.

Green things growing.

Even the air is better: earth and plants and so much sky.

No bitey dogs. No alarms. No electric fence zapping me.

Step, step and sniff.

Closer now. Curtains blow out the open front windows, house music pumping. Inside, they're dancing, they've been at it all night. She's in her bra and underwear, grinding against him. Roam is a housecat, one fat paw dangling over her shoulder. He's dressed in white: tight beater, cuffed pants, an untucked linen shirt. Greek statue come to life. Their bodies bump and slide, wrench apart in strange silhouettes, then plaster together, hungrily.

Not dead after all.

All the stones I carefully piled inside myself during his long absence shift, threaten to come crashing down in an avalanche of grief. I lean into the shadows of a sculpted bush until my heart slows. Right below the open window, and they still don't see me. My nails are ragged. The Chanel jacket, grimy, opens halfway to show skin.

Wish I'd showered.

My next step blocks the golden light, casting a grotesque shadow over them. Roam squints, sees me. He twirls so she faces the other way. She is singing and swinging her hips in lace panties.

Roam mouths: *what the fuck!*

Shoots the finger.

Truth is, Roam is even better looking. Put on a few pounds, all muscle. He's been eating well, fucking lots. My nostrils flare. Roam's true scent, the heated flesh, the sweat and effort of him, is gone. Also gone is the smell of the industrial laundry detergent used at the shelter, branding us wards of the state. His is a fancy trail of cake-batter and something woodsy, a sappy pine branch.

He cradles her close. Shakes his head at me, pleading silently.

For once he's afraid of losing something, too.

My fist clenches. This is what love does.

I set her purse on the window ledge.

Roam cocks his head; he doesn't recognize this once-elegant thing.

I shrug.

Rub the patch stuck to my chest, smooth the raggedy edges that threaten to peel.

Mackenzie peers over her shoulder, mid-song. She stares at me, at her purse. Confusion: eyebrows furrow. Then, slow mo: eyes dart, mouth slackens. She's not dumb. It's falling into place, one tick at a time. She points. Looks from me to Roam and back. "You know him? You planned this?" Then she's punching and slapping Roam.

He shields himself, says, "It's not how it looks."

Roam's mouth—sulky curves, black stubble hinting at an outline above. The tiny, dark trail under the bottom lip is moving.

What is he saying? I have no idea.

Whenever I've had enough of his bullshit, I press my lips tight, but Roam keeps kissing. Warm hands on my shoulders and neck, fingers in my hair, unhinge me. My jaw relaxes. My mouth, the traitor, opens. His tongue pushes, does all the work, and I just breathe.

Now it's his lips on hers, just the same.

The ground shifts, lawn quakes, rips apart. I wheeze air into my lungs.

Roam throws the fits; I grab the loot! Roam throws the—

"Stop," he shouts. At me, I think.

She is crying, black tears trace her pretty cheeks. She unzips the purse, dumps everything out, fingers what's left. Things are adding up, but still, she can't believe it.

I rip my pain patch in half, offer a piece to her over the windowsill while I flatten the other back on my clammy skin.

Just ask your insides, I want to say to her. Ask your belly and your bowels and your tormented liver for the truth. Mine, doomed as they are, always soften at his touch.

Oort Cloud Gets a Makeover

IT BEGINS with Plague House.

War, famine, pestilence, disease!

This, spray-painted on a rundown brownstone where a handful of resident environmentalists advocate counteracting overpopulation by any means necessary. Their slogans polarized last week's climate change protest—*bubonic, we want it*—and one kid caved from the social media backlash. Ergo a vacancy, and Jan's on it, the first to respond. It's the only place in town that strikes a chord as she combs the streets looking for a room to rent.

Twins answer the door. Or so Jan thinks.

"We're lovers," they announce, in matching striped shirts, denim overalls, thick eyeglass frames, and shorn hair. One is taller, the other slightly friendly. Both give Jan the once-over. Who knows what they see? Jan is a solid mass obscured by dark, baggy clothing; she is thick hair curtained across her unknowable face. She has come from some backwater village in the farthest reaches of the solar system; for college, for a life.

They say, "We need someone extreme. We're not that into humans."

"Ditto," says Jan.

They say, "Are you a cop? Full disclosure, we'll be doing a background check."

The friendly one shows Jan around and the tall one lurks, arms crossed, glaring.

The catastrophic kitchen: a congealed porridge pot presides over the splattered stove, hieroglyphs of pasta, flung and cemented, a red-sauce crime scene. The pantry reveals a grenade gone off, no survivors. Piled on the counter, the kitchen table, are pressure cookers of all sizes, test tubes, a large timer, a rat's nest of wire.

"Special project," says Frowny, stepping in front to shield the mess from Jan.

"There's a microbiologist in the basement, us on the top floor, and the vacant room above the kitchen beside Saffy. She's on a Buddhist retreat. We're vegan recyclers," Friendly says, pointing to a bin labeled *worms*. "We dumpster dive for groceries Wednesdays and Saturdays, after dark."

Frowny says, "We're on a grey-water filtration system, so if you *must* shower, you get five minutes. Toilets are flushed at noon and midnight."

"Right," Jan says. She must have misheard.

Friendly and Frowny exchange glances.

"We didn't see you at the protest."

Jan's not sure which of them spoke—both are thin-lipped, emanating a quiet rage.

Frowny says, "The earth is dying. Do you even care?"

"I just got into town yesterday," Jan lies.

"Hmm," says one.

"Freshman," murmurs the other.

"We need consensus," says Frowny, showing Jan the door. "We'll call after the house meeting."

Which means more nights squatting on the front porch of her mother's cousin's house in the suburbs. Every morning, Jan wrangles onto teeming buses, endures an epic subway ride into the city proper—more faces than she's seen her whole life, all mired in the same stink. She wanders around viewing overpriced student rentals, getting lost, freaking out, reorienting herself in these streets full of beautiful, clean, organized people, despising all of them. She follows the river's edge, the city's sinister, oily bisector, which eventually winds right back to Plague House, of all places. She doesn't knock, just sits, fingers crossed. Shadows and figures sometimes animate the window gaps between unwashed curtains. Surely they can see her outside, demonstrating commitment. She wants this so badly.

It's a feeling. A needle pulling a long thread out from her guts, leading her.

"Pick me," Jan whispers to their neglected lawn, to the pigeons strutting across the crumbling stoop.

When hunger and despair threaten to defeat her, a bookended rush hour awaits, and she reverses the journey—slammed into wrinkled suits, briefcases battering her shins, besieged by angry armpits as their owners cling to the overhead support bar on bus, tram, and subway car.

Every night after dinner, after the fierce red sun does its disappearing act, blazing across the sky and smoldering into the western horizon, immolating all hope but not one of the day's disappointments, Jan curls under sleeping bag and blanket in the reclining lawn chair, her temporary bed, reading course outlines in the streetlamp's glow. She's in limbo—far from her dreary family, her unremarkable birthplace, yet still dormant, a sleeper agent.

Will it never begin?

One evening, her mother's cousin knocks on the inside of her own front door before stepping out to the porch. House lights spill soft and white around her, illuminating a trilling, slobbering, fattened baby on one hip, a growling, bitey Jack Russell terrier between her ankles. Her face is a dust rag, worn through. Shrieks and thunder come from inside the house—toy blocks toppling—a castle overthrown, a monarchy deposed. Lawlessness. Anarchy. Full-blown combat ensues between the other squalling children, three of them. Jan can't tell them apart.

Breeder, thinks Jan, pitilessly.

The cousin sighs. "A microbiologist called. Says you can move in whenever, cash up front."

Plague House.

Hail, Rota Fortunae!

Tick, tick, and turn: a spoke in the witch's wheel, creaking toward Jan's destiny.

The vacated bedroom is small but equipped with a new-ish futon and wardrobe, both abandoned by the previous tenant. Jan unpacks her suitcase, her knapsack. The window overlooks a scruffy yard where a large calico suns herself—a good omen. The electric kettle her mom gave her means Jan can make instant noodles in her room, which she does after unpacking. No sign of the roommates. In the repugnant bathroom, which smells worse than the fetid latrine at the veteran's hall back home, hangs a poster of hungry, solemn children with eyes that shine and haunt. *One flush equals seven gallons drinking water!* The toilet bowl, filled to an ominous level—the household's collective excrement—is more of an indoor outhouse. She'd rather go in the yard. Usually she ducks to avoid her reflection, but this mirror has been defaced, completely covered by an elaborate, demonic collage: cut-outs of politicians and porn stars with X's for eyes. Tits and cocks and religious symbols and stock exchange market trading graphs. Images of wildfire, oil spills, slaughtered animals, their hot blood melting ice caps into oblivion.

Heavy.

And yet, such a relief to not have to look at herself, at her dense forestry: hair shrouding abundant brows, dark lashes, the soft fuzz lining her upper lip. Her lump of a torso hidden in oversized shirt, amorphous sweater, loose-fitting jeans. Sneakers. Her mother complains she dresses like a ten-year-old boy.

Back in the bedroom, Jan discovers a note slipped under the door. *House meeting agenda item: please do not overuse electrical appliances. We can hear the kettle.*

"Wipe everything down with Lysol," her mother urges, when Jan calls with the good news from a payphone down the street.

"Right," Jan says. "A flammable compound made of ethanol. Which kills people, Mom. Not to mention the environmental destruction."

"Well, it kills germs, Honey. That's all I know."

If her mother ever sees this place, she'll call Public Health, have it condemned.

"Are you going to get your own phone?"

Worry pinches her mother's voice.

"Dunno," says Jan.

"Try to make friends. Maybe in your classes?"

"As if."

In gender studies, her Monday morning elective, most students look like the not-twins. More than a style thing, not just a look, it's ideological, communitarian—new concepts that corrode Jan's entire mental scaffolding, her internal wiring, like battery acid, leaving her shaky, confused. This will take time to process. Who didn't get the memo? A handful of basic ponytailed girls and two or three dudes dotting the room. There is the professor, angular and distracted, and Jan.

Twenty minutes late, *wha-bam*, the door kicks open, all heads spin, and lo, a bizarre figure bursts across the room in front of the professor, whose mouth drops in amazement. A triangular metal sieve rests on the intruder's gauze-wrapped head. Delicate rags whoosh around limbs and flutter as the creature fixes Jan in her sights. The effect is decidedly ghost-like. Hare Krishnas also come to mind, with their robes and sashes—Jan saw them hitting tambourines at the airport. Snorts and chortles pepper the lecture hall. The professor stutters, "S-settle down, now," and the sauntering intruder retorts, "I couldn't possibly, Professor," before surrendering to the empty spot directly in front of Jan.

The towering headdress blocks Jan's view. Amid stifling wafts of sandalwood and patchouli, the creature turns with a smirk. Eyebrows, shaved off completely, disorient Jan's brain as it tries to make sense of a human face. Gold pencil around eyes and lips; a gold symbol, perhaps a rune, painted in the centre of the forehead.

"Got a pen?"

The voice is deep, melodic.

Jan scrambles to locate one.

"Paper?"

Who comes to class without a laptop?

The Being, and Jan is leaning towards thinking of this entity as female although clearly there is a higher concept at work, one that her sheltered upbringing in a crap small town has absolutely *not* prepared her for, collapses the hinged table of Jan's desk, dumping Jan's things unceremoniously. Rocking as far back as the chair will go, she sprawls precariously against Jan's legs, pinning Jan in her seat. Tilts that gilded face so the adorned head rests in Jan's *actual* lap, heavy as a bowling ball. The sieve pushes against Jan's stomach. Her crotch.

Dry mouth, wet palms, not enough air squeezing into Jan's panicky lungs.

Classmates snicker but the Lounger doesn't budge.

Eyes closed—asleep, or, more likely, drugs?

Jan gasps, "Excuse me." Shakes what she hopes is a shoulder.

One upside-down eye opens like a cat's.

Jan says, "Get off? I don't even know you."

"You're Jan. I'm Saffy," she says, pressing a finger to Jan's astounded lips.

"Roomies."

The chair teeters, pitches forward, slams back into place. Saffy, now sitting up properly with her back to the bewildered Jan, begins scribbling furious notes with the borrowed pen, as if nothing were amiss.

This is how they meet.

Jan's life completely re-routed. A fated detour into an unknown galaxy.

After class, Saffy grabs Jan's arm. Says, "Come, thou."

Pulls Jan against the current in the swarming halls, away from the cafeteria, towards the nearest exit. Jan's stomach growls. Hundreds of students, yet a pathway clears: Saffy's freaky costume, her swashbuckling swagger. Jan's discomfort shifts to a kind of woeful pride, what a celebrity handler might feel in the wake of an aging, demented Hollywood star.

Outside, Saffy pops the lid off a vitamin bottle, swallows a few capsules with homemade kombucha from a stainless-steel thermos as they cross the manicured lawn. "This is a totally satisfying lunch," she says. "Many forms of algae hold all the nutrients we need. You want?"

Jan shakes her head. "I'm getting fries, later."

"You know, the Canada Food Guide is a lie."

"Totally."

Saffy leads through the warren of tiny side streets abutting the campus, and in through the door of an unassuming storefront. Chimes ring, and an elfin, white-haired woman waves from behind the cash. It's the local charity resale shop, smelling of mothballs and mildew and unwashed armpit. Unfazed, Saffy digs through rack after rack, scraping hangers, exclaiming and tacking things she likes on a separate stand for further consideration.

Saffy says, "What are pants, anyway, Jan? Colour. Texture. Shape. Break fashion down and you're left with *concepts*. It's why I make most of my own clothes." She appraises an orange, floor-length caftan. "This screams midsummer ritual sacrifice, doesn't it?"

Jan has no idea. She's watching a bulbous spider build a web across the decrepit bookshelf. It spins and drops, zips back up the sticky thread, drops again. It's on a mission.

Saffy says, "Jan, why aren't you looking?"

Jan shrugs. "I don't really need anything?"

"This isn't about needs, not exactly."

How can Jan say that wearing other people's clothes creeps her out? Other people's verboten parts basically rubbing through time and space against her own unsubstantiated body: gross. And yes, maybe some pleasant, non-diseased girl simply outgrew this pair of jeans and wanted to prolong their inevitable trip to a landfill, but *maybe not*. Maybe something totally awful happened. Maybe she's riddled with scabies or pus-filled, open-sore boils. Maybe the girl is *dead* and her bereaved parents had to truck all her things here, to rid their home of the interminable weight of loss in an attempt to move forward with their own grief-stricken, now meaningless, lives.

In the children's section, Saffy shrieks, "A talisman!" and drags a massive stuffed polar bear to the cash where, delighted, she receives an unexpected fifty percent off. What Saffy gets: a set of linen curtains, a fireplace poker, dozens of plastic rosaries in a plastic bag marked down to one dollar, and a man's wool overcoat, several sizes too large. She is buzzing. Saddled with two colossal bags, Saffy can't possibly carry the toy bear, whose girth is such that Jan's arms don't reach all the way around the middle. Fifteen, twenty pounds, compounded by their meandering return to campus, where Saffy heads to her philosophy seminar, ditching Jan with the bear.

"Wait," Jan yells, but Saffy says, "See you at home!"

Chem, Earth, Phys.

All 100 levels, back-to-back, in the afternoon.

All while paired to the enormous bear.

Packed hallways mean Jan rams into everyone, can't see where she's going, even trips down a flight of stairs, but luckily lands on the animal. Bear is sometimes knocked from her grasp in the hustle. Frat boys hoot as they bash and wallop him. A trio of girls coo *so cuuute*, stroking his fat belly as Jan breaches the throng. In class, Bear requires his own seat, provoking no end of commentary from the profs and other students. Excruciating. Jan abhors attention. Tingling in the pit of her belly: humiliation, dread. Also, hitherto unknown anticipation. She can't wait to get back to Plague House. To unload Bear, but also to see Saffy again.

Who has ever been this interested in Jan before?

No one, not even her parents.

At home, Jan waits forever on the front stoop, doodling in a notepad. Maybe Saffy has a night class or epic meeting with the International Socialist Subcommittee? Up in her room, Jan heats the illicit kettle for more noodles. A film-club screening, a spontaneous potluck dinner? Or what? Jan has zero social life; she has no idea how other people spend their time.

Evening limps along, dragging its dark, shaggy tail.

Snuffs out the moon and most of the stars.

Saffy does not come home.

An accident.

Saffy, steamrolled by one of the city's massive, juice-spewing garbage trucks.

Or a kidnapping.

Saffy, whose affable lunacy surely attracts maniacs, brutalized in a ditch.

Eventually, Jan's distress is eroded by a growing suspicion that Saffy has, in fact, merely forgotten her. In a furious instant Jan knows. And why not?

Jan is a nobody. A country hick.

Jan is a dog, gnawing hope like a soup bone.

Jan has always hated everyone.

She props Bear in the corner of her room. Thick lashes, and a clicking sound when the lids jiggle over large glass eyeballs. It's hard to sleep with him staring. What if he's crawling with bugs? Back on planet normcore, Jan's obsessive mother would agree. One reason you don't drag somebody else's crap home from the garbage. How to sterilize a polar bear? Jan would dump him in Saffy's room, but right after the elaborations on recycling policies comes the Plague House golden rule, an exercise in *active consent*: no entering other people's rooms.

Like a vampire, you have to be invited.

"Wake up."

Jan screams. Someone's hand covers her mouth and it takes a long horror-film moment before her darting eyes make sense of the blue-black. She's in her sleeping bag on the second-hand futon in her new room. Saffy kneels, her moonstone face floating above, her long white fingers silencing Jan.

"You scared me," gasps Jan.

Then, more petulant, "Where've you been?"

Saffy says, "I met a very interesting guy, pure maths, a total brain. What's up?"

Not bludgeoned by a serial killer.

Jan says, "Nothing. Anyway, Bear."

Saffy says, "Wow! Amazing!" as though she's never seen him before. She rocks him in her arms and inspects each dangling limb and especially his head.

"Let's take him apart," she says.

And Jan is following to her room at three in the morning.

Did Saffy have sex with the mathematician? Is Jan allowed to ask?

"First," Saffy says, "we have to cleanse this space."

"Now?"

Apparently, a requirement before launching any new project. Which means Jan is ritually mopping with rosemary floor wash while Saffy circles the room carrying a large shell with a smoking herb bundle. It's pungent, would set off a smoke detector if the house were equipped with one, which it isn't. Jan is startled by an intermittent gong—booming, reverberating—when Saffy introduces *vibrational sound* to the cleansing process. Saffy tilts her head as though awaiting a far-off signal, then fills the room with *the sacred syllable,* the universally chanted *OM*.

Lightheaded, Jan reclines on one of the bamboo mats Saffy uses in lieu of conventional furniture.

Go-ong.

"Will that wake the others?" asks Jan.

"Maybe. But it'll release deeply rooted negativity," says Saffy.

First, the decapitation.

Despite Jan's resentment at lugging Bear around all day, she feels badly when his head rolls across the floor and stops at her feet. Those accusing eyes. That sad little stitched-on mouth. Saffy wants Jan to remove the stuffing from his head while she opens a seam running the length of the body. Soon they have a sagging head and limp torso. They collect the fluffy guts in a bag for a future project. Saffy slips the bearskin around her shoulders. She's altering it into some kind of suit.

Saffy says, "It's a revolutionary act for a sensitive, conscious person to even *exist.* I believe fashion can serve Truth as a manifesto. That's basically my thesis."

Jan says, "Why draw so much attention, though? Seems exhausting."

Saffy says, "You aren't like them. Why pretend?"

"You think I look like other people?"

That's a first.

"No. But have you realized your karmic role? Are you on your perfect path?"

Jan thinks, nonsense. Says, "You want me to copy you?"

Saffy's face, a garage door, rolls shut.

Saffy says, "That'd also be a lie. First year's hard, but you'll discover your own purpose. Clothing reinforces, helps keep focus."

"So what are you?" says Jan.

"High Priestess. Obviously."

Jan asks, "Does it bother you that people think you're nuts?"

"What is sanity? A declaration of conformity. Who wants that?"

"Who wants to be locked up?" says Jan.

"No one's locking anyone up," says Saffy. "Not yet, anyway."

While Saffy runs her sewing machine—using who knows how many kilowatts—Jan traces the length of Bear's claws with a finger.

Jan has known this strange girl less than twenty-four hours and here she is, lounging on a newly mopped floor, *in her bedroom*, chatting away as though they've been friends for yonks. Silly to have been upset earlier; like her mom says, that's insecurity talking! Jan's in pyjamas, wrists to ankles, but if she tilts her head she can see her putrid feet, a pair of flopping fish. She scrunches them. Should have pulled on socks. Saffy, on the other hand, wears only what amounts to a see-though slip, one pink nipple peeping out as she moves her arms to catch up the bobbin thread, as she feeds the fussy cloth under the needle. It's as though at some point in the day, like a snake, Saffy sheds her layers.

Perhaps they are strewn about the mathematician's lair.

Jan is afraid of crossing the invisible line, invading privacy, but also sex weirds her out—talking about it, at least. Not like she's ever done it much. There was the zitty boy at science camp, a nauseating and awkward make-out session, whose premature crescendo landed on the pages of her open textbook.

Saffy says, "Who did you hang out with in high school? Art fags or jocks?"

That F-word, again, chafing her.

Jan says, "I'm not much of a joiner."

The scuzzy lunchroom, smell of old soup, euchre games at the nerd table. Two notable classmates: Klaus, a sassy, born-again yearbook editor who ghosted her after prom, and Lisa, who moved out east for musical theatre. Now their chats feel stilted, pointless—reminders of all the things Jan wants expunged from her life. Jan is desperate to become totally unrecognizable. To become.

Jan says, "Do you meet guys easily?"

Saffy stops sewing.

"I meet *whomever* seems interesting. Don't you?"

"No, actually," says Jan. "I don't usually talk to anyone."

"Hmm," says Saffy. "You're dark matter; things fly at you, stick to you. Don't you find? You're carrying so much."

Jan's not sure.

She's tired a lot of the time.

Alone.

"I didn't fuck Math Man. Is that what you want to know?" Saffy smiles, making Jan feel childish. "Sex isn't the only way to connect. Anyways, I'm dating a Satanist. You kind of remind me of him."

"Uh," says Jan.

"Okay, what do you think?"

Saffy presents Bear, utterly transformed into an empress's long cape. Bear's head sits properly on her skull, his snout shielding her eyes, while his lower jaw rides the bones of her clavicle perfectly. Like he bit off her head—a reciprocal amputation—and holds it neatly between his fearsome teeth. Elegant, twisted haute couture.

"This will be worn at a momentous gathering, a future press conference," Saffy says.

"Wow," says Jan.

Dawn comes creeping. Rosy beams penetrate the dirty window, the room, setting the girls alight. Saffy is brilliant, Jan knows. Whacked in the head, but a total genius.

Saffy has occasional late-night dates with the Satanist, usually at his apartment across town. She very rarely lets him crash at Plague House, refuses to even let him keep a toothbrush in the dirty cup by the sink, which is fine by Jan. He is only ever an extra set of socked feet padding the hallway to the bathroom, a baritone murmur on the other side of the bedroom wall, a forgotten black T-shirt that stinks like a regular boy, not an unholy beast, after all.

It's Jan who knows Saffy best.

Chugging from a cheap bottle of wine, Saffy confides: she was born on a ship in the Baltic Sea, abandoned by her unwed mother, adopted by grandparents and, shockingly, gambled away in a poker game by her drunken grandfather. Probably why she is innately suspicious of others—despite being rescued by the grandmother, who marched directly to the neighbours' home and seized the bewildered toddler from a hearthside cot. "The damage was already done," Saffy says in a sad voice.

Jan totally gets it.

She reaches, slow motion.

Strokes the knitted sleeve of Saffy's sweater.

September and October threaten November. Jan hardly ever calls home. She's busy. School, plus she's happy, for once. Letters addressed in her mother's cheerful cursive arrive, but Jan chucks them on the wardrobe, unopened. The girls' routine: orbiting the arts and science buildings by day, hitting up a particularly dreary café with remarkable drink specials after class, then picnicking along the brackish river, consuming the crisp and wholesome autumn evenings.

Inseparable, for the most part.

Nights, house meetings, they work out details of their impending plan. Argue about the target endlessly. They're fed up with government inaction. They want a metaphor. They want results.

Saffy has monitored their polluted river, which supplies the city's drinking water, for three years, trying to rouse local citizens to speak up, to care. Levels are even higher now, and aside from the trembling of striders and flies, aside from the occasional splash—a fish, a frog, something—and the stirred reflection from a tender breeze, the water is relatively stagnant. Green scum collects around protruding dead branches—bare arms with long, accusatory fingers, all that remains visible of dozens of uprooted trees that collapsed into the river from flooded banks.

Pamphlets, letter writing, petitions, protest—nothing works.

They're doing direct action now; strategic, vivid, merciless.

Jan takes house-meeting minutes in pig Latin, is sworn to burn, eat, or otherwise destroy them in the event of a raid, before they fall into the wrong hands. *Phase one:* the intrepid microbiologist (ete-Pay), a shaggy-haired pill-popper, discovered a bacterial sample that Jan released into the abetting river, near the filtration plant. *Check.* Mass symptoms, vomiting and diarrhea, should be making headlines forthwith. *Phase two:* the not-twins assembled an improvised device (omb-bay) from online instructions. City hall, *not* the shopping centre. *Check check.* It'll be Jan's job to detonate: set things in motion.

Everyday it's getting closer. There'll be no turning back.

Saffy says she believes in Jan.

Jan *thinks* she's ready.

"What happens after?" asks Jan.

"You might get arrested," say the not-twins, "or taken in for questioning."

"You'll have to stay strong, not rat out the rest of us," they say.

Frankly, Jan is more concerned about the device malfunctioning, blowing off fingers or worse. She supresses an image of her disfigured, bandaged face, her uncomprehending, weeping mother.

"You're so brave," Saffy says, draping an arm around Jan's shoulders, squeezing.

Jan inhales Saffy's animal scent, the hint of patchouli. Sees beauty at every turn, for once. Even in the filthy, anti-establishment basement where they meet. Even in this cruel, bourgeois city, and definitely on their romantic, doomed riverbank. Light and colour bleed into Jan's grey landscapes, livening them, heating a central spot inside her chest, filling it.

What else Jan knows about Saffy: she's a poised and agile catalyst, erudite, with penetrating intellect and forceful views. Utterly at ease in her body. Charismatic, able to level an opponent with linguistic and philosophical tripwires, devastating the inferior argument with precision, her composure completely intact.

Saffy will be their public face.

On the riverbank, high above their spread blanket, a dozen corvids screech and circle—chasing, dipping, gliding. They're rallying around the imposter, a blinking white drone supposedly programmed by a local news channel to scoop rush-hour traffic reports. It appears every afternoon and buzzes with the mechanical whine of a large hive, louder than a thousand bees. Saffy and Jan wear dollar-store Halloween masks to scramble the drone's facial-recognition software, in case. On the other side of the river is a public park where a large black dog barks, barks, then stops. There are the birds gargling above, and the drone, and the wind tossing the silvery leaves of the trees.

Jan is probably in love.

Saffy shakes a cereal box, dumps a technicolour pile of Fruit Loops onto the grass. She's made cereal-coated gauntlets from a duct-tape base and wants a matching choker to wear with Empress Bear tonight. Down at the library, Jan's classmates are studying for a chemistry midterm. But not Jan. Jan is nauseous, on the precipice, about to scandalize the entire Western world: *phase two*. She glances at the Hello Kitty knapsack, pink-and-white treachery, resting several feet away. In a few minutes, Saffy will go home to change and Jan will carry the bag directly to city hall, alone.

Saffy says, "Personally, I can't wait 'til humans are wiped out and nature overtakes the planet—goodbye, concrete."

Jan imagines a dark forest sharpening and gnashing its branches, uncoiling long, thorny vines that grasp and reclaim all the old wood abandoned by a lost humanity: floorboards and roof beams and church pews. All of it.

Jan says, "What do you see when you look at me?"

"The void."

"Great," says Jan, glum.

"No, listen, it's brilliant. You really don't give a shit," says Saffy, stringing one fruity circle at a time. "Sometimes I wish I was more like that."

Jan says, "My mom thinks I'm depressed."

"Ha. A totally rational response to a fucked-up world. Society is disgusting."

Jan says, "Yeah. I mean, I agree. Just ... so what."

"Exactly! If there was an award for Most Apathetic and, I mean, obviously there never will be, you'd be a prime candidate. It's not a typically feminine response."

"Neither is wearing a saucepan on your head," says Jan.

Saffy laughs. "It's an industrial strainer, the closest thing to a medieval helmet I could find. I need protection. My ideas are under attack!"

"No kidding."

Saffy says, "Finished. Tie me up?"

Jan blushes.

"My necklace, perv," says Saffy.

Jan, mortified, tries not to screw up. Her clumsy fingers tie a knot at the back of Saffy's bent neck. Saffy is bareheaded, for once, hair buzzed short. There's the dip at the base of her skull, like a thumbprint, and the knobby pearls at the top of her spine.

"Seems like you're hiding inside yourself," says Saffy, gently.

Jan says, "You mean there's a skinny person hiding inside my fat?"

"No. That is *not at all* what I meant. This is about the energetic presence of your primal self. It's buried. What if you allowed it to fill you up and radiate outward?"

"That will never happen," says Jan.

"I'm so serious. Let's cut your hair."

"Now?"

Jan has never known anyone like Saffy. Lick a nine-volt battery and you get a small shock, you pay attention. That's what it is to be near her. And what if she's right? What if there is some other way to exist, to move through this hideous repetition of day after day? To live, even to die, with meaning?

Saffy says, "Oh, what the hell. Masks off."

She wields a gleaming pair of scissors from her sewing kit. Flicks Jan's hair with the dubious river water. Forces a comb through Jan's dense, tangled mess.

"Ready? Let's find you."

Snip.

Snip.

Snip.

Curls drop in the grass around Jan, who sits cross-legged with eyes pinched shut.

Jan says, "You're cutting off a lot."

"Only what's absolutely necessary," says Saffy.

"Maybe it was okay the way it was?"

"No, Jan, it wasn't. Your inner essence was strangled by that hair. Et voilà! Baby bangs, very Betty Page. This will change everything."

"I feel sick," says Jan.

"Shh," says Saffy.

Fingertips whisk away the tiny, loose hairs, dance across Jan's forehead, cheeks, nose, and chin. Tug and fluff the still-long parts of her hair. Saffy can do anything as long as she doesn't stop touching, igniting fiery trails along Jan's scalp that shiver into gooseflesh on her neck and arms and elsewhere.

Saffy whispers, "Open your eyes, Jan."

Jan does, is blinded.

A paradisiacal blast, late afternoon sunbeams emanating from behind Saffy, blotting her out; just her silhouette and the radiating mandoria, white-gold like the Virgin of Guadalupe, like any holy prophet come with a message. Sunspots swim and smear and Jan's eyes tear up, which she pretends is caused by UV rays and not by the unbearable aching inside, at the sudden appearance of the Divine, whose existence she has denied since childhood.

"Shit, Jan, it's really good. You look totally believable."

Saffy snaps photos for after, when the media will ask.

Saffy curls close and Jan drinks her in: the sloping, regal nose; pretty bow mouth and generous bottom lip; delicate ears, silver hoops piercing them like the grasping talons of a small, angry bird. The mask, gone, but the pull of its strap against her cheekbones mapped by red indentations.

Jan sees Saffy, and the reverse must also be true.

Nowhere to hide, no hood on her jacket, no scarf, it's not quite toque season. Jan is bare, she may as well be totally naked out here in the grassy strip that traces the tainted river.

An inch, maybe less, between them. Breathing the same charged air. Parts of Saffy's body press against parts of Jan's body and those are the places that roar, that speed away from themselves, blazing and burning, a powerful solar flare. Those are the parts now singing an alien song, ripping open the earth beneath her, flinging ancient icy chunks, asteroids and meteoroids and unnamed debris, pell-mell, into the powerful central star, into the sun.

Four-Letter Word for "Loose"

"FEVER'S UP," says Carole in her cigarette-sogged voice. "Gotta get a line in and hydrate the little bugger."

Fluorescent lights gleam on the tiled walls of the emergency clinic. It smells of dirty boy and chemical disinfectant and the sucrose-sweetened Nicorette gum clamped between Carole's stained molars. She tugs her limp, greying hair. God, that stylist took a lot—she's practically bald. Rolls the sleeve of her over-sized sweater, straightens the sheets gathered in a damp pile around the boy's heaving torso. Each laboured breath lifts him from the sweat-soaked mattress. Pain ripples, the bedrails tremor.

"Norm, better grab the ree-strains. Kid's kicking up a storm."

Norm's baggy scrubs drag under the worn heels of his orthopaedic sneakers, shushing like wind in a leafy tree. He scratches his mid-life belly, unconfined by the green cotton. He sighs. Swishes burnt coffee from the vending machine down the hall in his *Orderlies Do It in Scrubs* mug.

"Can you hear me, Hoofy?"

"What kind of name is that?" asks Norm.

Carole shrugs and peers into the boy's slack face with its kohl-lined eyes, mascara-thickened lashes curled like the fat legs of a spider. Hoofy's eyes open and roll, lids flutter. Carole remembers the initial strangeness of the name. But after getting to know him, it fit. Hoofy is a bit feral, like some woodland creature from a fairy tale.

"What, he huffs glue?"

"Norm, for chrissakes, grab his file. I'm dosing him."

"It's called a coffee break, Carole, every five hours. It's the law."

Norm sighs again, dramatically. He opens a dog-eared folder from the wobbly stack on the side table. With one hand he flicks the pages. With the other he opens the cupboard above the table and feels for the restraints.

"What have you got?" she says.

He says, "Terrific. Paramedics picked him up at the shelter, so nada."

"Who's the emergency contact?"

"Boyfriend. He's positive, a carrier, refused treatment. I already called, sounds like he's partying. Asshole hung up on me. Oh, and there's your card." Norm snorts.

"Poor little shit," she says.

Carole had first seen Hoofy almost two years ago, panhandling beside the subway station on her way to work. Out of habit she had elbow-clamped her purse, pretended not to hear, then pretended not to have change. There were hundreds just like him visiting the clinic, thousands more on the street or in shelters. She had rules, boundaries being vital in this line of work—give no cash, share no personal information, bring no work home. But something about Hoofy wormed through her defences, into her soft tissue, the vital organs. His eyes hooked you. Those dark circles—drugs, fatigue, illness, and something else, something glittering—

haunted her throughout the work day and again later, once she was home in her three-bedroom apartment, legs up on the coffee table, drinking chardonnay. Under the dirt and grease and suspicion, the boy was so young. What, fourteen? Same as her kids.

He was huddled there the next day, too, and on impulse she handed over her lunch of leftover pasta. From then on, every morning she lined up a third brown bag on the kitchen counter beside the twins' high-protein sandwiches, energy bars, peelable fruit. Homemade cookies, once in a blue moon. She'd tucked her business card with the clinic address inside, and so it began. Most days she didn't see him, and gave his lunch away. But Hoofy's erratic visits to the clinic meant that she was building trust, *rapport*—helping, at least a bit.

Carole says, "There's a mother somewhere."

Once or twice the kid had talked about his early years, the shithole he'd crawled out of.

"Whitby. Maybe Oshawa? Find her."

Norm rolls his eyes. "Do I look like Magnum P.I.?"

"Just do it. Call the shelter, social worker might know. While you're at it, page that freaking on-call doctor."

He says, "You're kidding, right?"

She mutters, "When's the last time I cracked a joke?"

Norm's phone rings in his chest pocket, the intro to the long-ago dance hit *La Bamba*. He fumbles to silence it.

"Get," Carole says, and Norm swishes out the door.

"Bonehead," she mutters.

She hates doing rounds with Norm. In her more paranoid moments, Carole suspects a set-up—that the supervisor schedules them together on purpose, hoping to push her over the edge. Have her quit in a rage or do something regrettable, give them a reason to fire her.

Hoofy moans. Carole fills a syringe and taps air bubbles from the chamber. Her twins, Ryan and Raquel, will be sixteen next month, but are taller, more filled-out than Hoofy. Sheltered, better fed. Raquel is good at French and Spanish. Ryan is into hockey, although they can't afford the equipment. He outgrows it within the season and then there's another whopping bill. Carole does what she can on one salary. The twins are fairly directionless but have school and friends and one shift a week at the neighbourhood movie theatre.

Not addicts. Not street trade.

"Who's your daddy," she says. She strokes Hoofy's clammy brow. Those eyes—two black stones, mahogany in the light. So like Ernesto's. No wonder the kid got to her.

Guapa, he called her, and so she was, with Ernesto's arm around her waist on a dance floor the drunken night they met. So fast. His calloused hands balanced her on the handrail of the fire escape behind the bar where they fucked, careless, losing one of her heels in the process. Barefoot, she took him home. God, she wasn't even young, already thirty, but unattached and starved for adventure. Ernesto propped open the door to an unrestricted Cuban universe. Music like she'd never heard—Spanish guitar and African drums: congas, batá, claves, and cajón. Sloppy gulps of rum and so much sex. Ernesto cooked tubers marinated in mojo, fried plantains, dulce de leche. They were broke and mostly ate rice and sofrito black beans. "It's you and me," he'd say, smiling. "Moros y Cristianos." They married at city hall, cajoling an urban planner on his lunch break to be their witness.

Soon Carole was doing the cooking. Less sex and no music. Tensions escalated. "Greedy Guapa," he called her, despite pouring her savings into his favourite bottles, a new car, vacations, gifts for relatives back home. Priorities, she thought. "Culture clash," Ernesto said. "Language and class and your white white lies, Guapa." Ernesto was not *much* darker than she, not in the summer, not with her spray tan—or so she thought. His mother, he once revealed, was a German tourist who'd lived some years with his horn-player father before leaving, never to be seen again. Carole preferred to minimize their differences and changed the topic whenever he railed against discrimination in her cold, unwelcoming country. Back then she believed love precluded prejudice, could offset a centuries-old pain.

Ernesto said, "You don't understand shit."

What Carole learned: even a nurse cannot suture the wounds of the motherless.

Then came the twins. The credit freeze. Carole couldn't diagnose the sickness seeping from Eduardo's pores: frustration, a growing sense of futility, despair. The other woman, also pregnant, heralded their inevitable divorce—how cliché. Years later, Carole's still paying off the interest. Beyond lax, Ernesto, now living at large, takes deadbeat to a new level: zilch for child support, birthday cards come late or not at all. Once in a blue moon he materializes on their doorstep, demanding to see the twins. They see-saw between curiosity, longing, and moody resentment where their father is concerned. They need a male role model, especially Ryan, but who? A middle-aged numbing of the doomed triangle below her hips means she can, finally, ignore sex. As for Eduardo, she snuffed out every last flicker of feeling she had for the man. It was the only way.

Carole's phone vibrates deep in the pocket of her long, belted cardigan. A text from Raquel, *we're studying at Rob's tonight.*

Lies.

Carole texts back, *Not a chance kiddo. See you both at home.*

Exclamation points, indignant through repetition, a flurry of emoticons letting her know what a B$7CH F@C3 CVNT she is.

It hurts, but Carole's instincts are spot-on. The proof is in the kids' vitriol, which confirms they'd planned something more exciting. Probably Ryan using Raquel's phone, although lately Raquel is as bad-tempered, as crude as her brother. They come by it honestly. Eduardo was never one to mince words. Nowadays, neither does Carole.

In fact, Carole is a hard-ass, everyone says so, especially at work. Hence the healthy-communication coaching she was required to do after her recent altercation with the night-shift leader. (Carole was right, but the shift leader's feelings got hurt.) She can't drop her guard with the twins, not for a minute. Tough love is the only thing keeping them on track. Carole's reoccurring dream: a tightrope strung high above a rocky cliff, the twins trotting along it, and she, desperate, running back and forth in the grass at one end. She, barking like a mad dog, begging them to not slip, to not fuck up. The twins say she's a control freak, but overdosing teens get wheeled into the clinic every day of the week, puking up lethal concoctions of pharmaceuticals and drain cleaner, booze and pills. Half the pills come from the family medicine cabinet. Parents are usually the last to know anything, but not Carole.

Once, Ryan's feet were so tiny Carole popped them in her mouth. The warm neck scent, the sheer delight she got from rubbing their round tummies, enraptured her. Utterly dependent, they were incapable of betrayal.

Vibrations, more vibrations, then her phone starts ringing.

The whining is hard to take. Worse, when they gang up: one softens her, being *nice*, 'til she discovers it's a premeditated cover for the other. When they hiss *yuma* and *puta gringa*—that cuts deep. Conjures Eduardo's enduring accusations, their great racial divide. The rare times the twins fight each other, it's a bloodbath. Words splinter like shrapnel, rapid-fire door slamming, heavy-metal artillery blasting from Ryan's room, hip-hop assaults from Raquel's. In those moments, Carole is like a United Nations volunteer, forced to patrol the frontlines, hands covering ears, tiptoeing forgotten landmines. So far, no communication tips have helped. Frankly, she prefers being the bad guy.

Carole silences the phone, drops it back in her pocket. One new thing she's trying: not saying the first words that want to fly out her mouth. "That's called adulting," said Jenny, the pastel-wearing twenty-three-year-old employee-assistance counsellor. "No shaming, no blaming," she sing-songed, waggling a finger at Carole. "Let's try using 'I' statements. Like, *I need, I feel.*"

Carole's other hand goes to the opposite pocket from habit, feeling for the lighter. Shit. She forgot she's quitting, again.

Ryan tried to teach her to vape, which he refers to as a *douche-flute*. Not encouraging, and it felt eerily futuristic: an Orwellian boner kill. It's cigarettes or nothing, she's decided.

What she really needs—*I need*—is a fresh piece of the medicated gum, but it's in her purse at the nursing station, in her mini-locker under the desk. Carole counts from ten backwards, runs out of air at seven. Starts over. Another of Jenny's suggestions for a *win-win outcome*. Basically, not saying what you think. Two framed degrees on the wall behind Jenny's wide desk. She has zero job experience, unless you count babysitting and working summers as a lifeguard at the local pool. Carole knows, she used to drop the twins there for Saturday lessons. How could she confide in a child, one so blandly privileged? But the union was clear. If Carole demonstrates she's a *team player*, she might avoid disciplinary action.

Hoofy groans and twists the bedsheets, teeth chattering. Carole has never seen him so weak. Hep C, who knows what else. She's pulled blood work, should have results soon. She'd rather talk to this damaged kid who's already survived unfathomable hardship. Surely that amounts to something, some kind of street wisdom or strength of character? Could so much suffering really be in vain?

When Jenny asked her to *pinpoint* her workplace stressors on a *pyramid chart*, Carole laughed out loud. For a brief moment she imagined actually unleashing one loathsome secret after another on the girl—the graphic horrors of frontline work: gunshot wounds, overdoses, botched suicides; tragic stories whispered in confidence. The cruel symptoms of poverty and racism—words and concepts she no longer shrinks from—demons stalking her patients since childhood. Hell, even her light-skinned children are impacted. She imagined unveiling her own suffering, working in this misery industry. The whole single-parent saga, raising teens alone, chronic money problems, terminal loneliness, and, buried deep down, the infinite rage—her inner fuel—glowing like a white-hot coal. Violent impulses—to vanquish, to destroy by fire—overwhelm Carole when she sits across from young Jenny. This fledgling social worker, so like the idiot girl Carole used to be, knows everything and nothing at the same time.

Norm sags against the closed door and checks his phone, yawning. The baby cried until four, then screamed again for milk at five-thirty. Alison nurses in bed with the light on. "You're not sleeping if I can't," she says. More texts. *Need dia-*

pers. Pls pick up! Plus voice messages; it takes time to key in the password, listen to the automated coaching, and then to Alison's sighs and the sharp pinch of her voice. It sounds like she hates him, like he's terminally stupid. Texting is better. He can imagine a relaxed tone, something supple. The truth is she resents Norm more now that he's given her what she said she always wanted. This whole baby thing is a regrettable plunge down a gloomy elevator shaft; Norm is falling, falling past fatigue and fear and endless shit-smeared diapers, toward certain annihilation.

He tucks the phone in his pocket, a warm rectangle protecting his left ventricle.

At the nursing station, he hovers over Stephanie's desk and she clears her screen with a tap of acrylic nails. Loose tendrils of hair cling to her neck. Her collarbone is lit, V-neck accentuating plump breasts, their cleft dark and sweet, drawing his eyes down between them. She smells like honey-custard tarts.

"Updating your profile?" he says.

"Maybe." She swings her chair to face him. "Don't tell the Borg." Stephanie's eyes are lined in three shades of bruise, her lips glossed to high finish. "She still on rounds?"

"Yeah," he says. "Wants intel on a half-dead kid."

"What's in it for me?" asks Stephanie.

"Anything you want, baby."

"You're too easy," she says, laughing.

Stephanie grabs the patient file from Norm, reaches for a pen from the jar she keeps near her monitor. Drawstring pants stretch tight across her rump.

Norm swallows. Carole, aka the Borg, says Steph tailors her uniforms to fit, that it's scientifically impossible to look good in hospital garb. He has to agree. Hundreds of women, all day, every day, sagged into the same shapeless cotton, some stuffed like sausage into its casing. Only Steph looks like she materialized from a music video, a casting couch, a porn shoot.

Images of Steph tease him when he lies in bed at night, and also when he showers, lathering thick pubic hair, thighs, erect penis. Just this morning he'd fantasized bending her over, tearing her scrubs, and plunging himself into her, again and again. He imagined pressing her face into the desk as he thrust, and, in so doing, achieved the most powerful orgasm, one that left him gasping and light-headed for several minutes, until the water ran cold. Had he been too loud? *Yes!* So said Alison's stony glare when he finally emerged from the bathroom, waist wrapped in a towel. She cringed when he kissed her forehead on the way out the door. Like he was a criminal, a sex offender, and not simply her blue-balled husband, an average man with a few basic needs.

"Vamoose," Steph says, flicking her nails.

Unsmiling, she says, "I mean it."

Norm coughs. How long has he been standing there straining his Hanes, mouth hanging slack?

"Busy tonight?" His voice tremors slightly.

She meets his eyes, unblinking.

"Clubbing with my hot boyfriend," she says.

Safer to stick with the Borg, Norm thinks, and heads back the way he came.

Has Alison ever referred to *him* as her hot boyfriend? Probably not even back when she was actually into him. Last weekend, morose, Norm drank half a case of beer and called his older brother. Ken, a father of three, works in finance and is a bit of a blowhard. They hadn't talked in months, not since the baby. Norm slurred, "How do you fucking do it?" Ken had advised, "Take turns getting sleep. Be considerate. Basically, grow the fuck up, Norman."

Norm ducks into the staff lounge, aka the Henhouse. He needs a proper coffee. A half-dozen nursing aides liven the place, laughing and arguing over the daily crossword. "Hey Norm," they say, and return to the newspaper, which covers a good portion of the lunch table. Ponytails flick; there's wild gesturing and a scramble to fill in an answer. Norm dumps the dregs into the sink and rinses his mug. Pours hot coffee, adds cream, sugar, just the way he likes. Leans against the counter to sip it. "What's a four-letter word for loose?" asks Tahmina, and Norm, without pausing, says, "Slut." Gales of laughter. Svetlana swats his forearm. "How's the baby?" she says, and her pretty, made-up eyes linger on his. "Great. Every time she looks at me, she screams." He's joking, sort of. He has an aversion to the baby's smells, hates touching her, holding her. Alison is forcing the issue, accusing him of some kind of phobia. Svetlana smiles; her pink oval nails rake his skin. Goosebumps, hairs rise up. "Oh, she will love her Daddy, don't worry." He's heard it's a turn-on for some women, having a fertility track record. So that's one thing.

"Aren't you on rounds with the Borg?" says Tahmina, and he goes, "Yep," and raises his steaming mug in a cheer, which cracks them all up. They hoot, "Go, go, before she reports you!" Norm slips out to the hall but doesn't move, not right away. He soaks up their muffled voices through the thick door: soprano exclamations and alto rumblings—Svetlana, he thinks—and in this moment Norm feels good, redeemed.

Glory days.

As in his sophomore high school year, when he was muscled and lean and had great hair. He was the rising football star and dated any girl he liked, until a torn anterior cruciate ligament forced him to the sidelines, crutched and limping, waiting for reconstruction surgery. Before the long year of rigorous rehabilitation, in which he privately battled depression and mood swings as he watched the rest of the team go on to regional champions without him. His marks sucked, but up until that point nobody cared. He was sure to be scouted for a college team, everyone said so. Had to devise a back-up plan due to the now limited range of motion in the finally healed knee joint. His dream, crushed. His future, disintegrated.

Alison was not his usual, lewd type. He hadn't even noticed her until she began tutoring him. She used to arrive promptly, ringing the bell at his parents' suburban home, soundlessly toeing her sneakers onto the boot tray. Her small mouth pursed when she looked over a math problem, tried to follow his logic in arriving at the wrong answer. She didn't make him feel bad. Didn't nag, not then. He began to notice things: her perfume, the shine of her lightly glossed lips, the way her faded jeans rode her hips. Once, when her neckline was uncharacteristically open—a neglected or lost button—he craned his head to follow the shadow defining her breasts, to catch a glimpse of the lace on her bra straps, on the brassiere itself. She'd done it on purpose to excite him, he later decided. Lured him, unsuspecting, and he'd fallen for it.

Whatever.

Somewhere along the way Alison tired of flattering him and a new woman emerged: irritable, dull to his charms, no longer easy. He recently overheard her on the phone telling her sister that he'd never have been hired if there weren't a shortage of male nurses. Like a face slap. Back when he'd gotten the job, Alison had made a special roast and invited his parents for dinner. They'd opened a good bottle of wine and toasted his success. For weeks after, each time he punched the clock at the end of his shift, a dumb grin broke over his face. Now he's not sure how to feel. He's stuck, coasting in his dull routine. Norm hates the term "nurse," is pleased when people mistake him for a doctor or surgeon, which happens almost every day. But the money isn't bad, there are benefits of course, and the pension, well, that's what they're all waiting for.

Norm returns to the clinic's emergency wing and catches the Borg sitting on the edge of the bed, talking. Not in her usual robot voice. God, is she crying? He can't wait to tell them at the Henhouse. He passes her the file.

"Beamsville," she croaks, and wipes Hoofy's bruised arm with antiseptic. "That's where he's from."

She aims for skin that's not already scabbing, not infected, oozing pus. Morphine pushes from needlepoint into the kid's bloodstream.

Norm says, "Bet he's really digging that morphine."

Carole says nothing, uncharacteristically.

Norm wonders if she's having a stroke or, finally, the crack-up everyone has predicted.

"Uh, Carole? Everything okay?"

She turns, looking intensely, really *seeing* him, all of him, which causes him to falter. Says, "One day, your little girl could be in trouble. If she's lucky, someone might be there to help. *I hope* it's not an underachieving dickshit like you, Norm."

Carole says brightly, "Think I'm getting the hang of these 'I statements.'"

Meanwhile, morphine, morphine.

Morphine drips and surges in Hoofy's bloodstream, pulls him back to the Otherworld. To his deep dreaming of the sun-drenched Don Valley, where he and some of the other kids burrow in pissed-out territories, wild as fur-bearers, camping rough in the shadow of the overpass—that great steel arch hanging above the valley, cleaving it in two.

Sun pokes treetops, into the valley and beyond, toward the cityscape. Cars honk and speed and stall their way over the monster bridge carrying them to the cluster of grey towers that pierce the brightening sky.

Hoofy assumes his true form—a hare—crouched in the warm grass beside a patch of his favourite bell-shaped flowers: harebells. Stems drip white sap. Hoofy licks. They're sweet with a bitter aftertaste. This is medicine. The earth's own hot smell laid open. The creek sings. Ferns unfurl. A bee stumbles past, drunk on nectar. Hoofy grooms his brown limbs and licks the fur between his large, clawed toes, calming himself. He is safe here, in the sweet nest he dug out last spring.

Free.

Hoofy noses a red-brown parade: ants, single file. A spider spindles fallen twigs past a yellow-and-black-striped snail, whose slick trail boasts its journey up the milkweed's stem and into the white web of its lair, where a horsefly writhes uselessly, bound by silky thread. Moles tunnel deep in the earth, worms churn, and the soil releases life's powerful essence. Clay and loam, mulch and rot. Invisible organisms eat their way through, transforming it. Wind rattles the poplars. Wind shimmies the sumac and wild raspberry. Wind carries sulphuric burps and billows from the stagnant pond. Violet patches of harebell whisper a warning.

Hoofy hops, nostrils trembling, ears tall.

Thumps a strong back foot on the ground.

Silver on white, shadows flit. A slow sky circling.

Cloud?

He freezes. Cold veined, his bowels cramp.

Whiteness reminds him of that elusive world beyond dreaming, that other time and place: antiseptic tiles, shining tools, sharps. Voices and lights and pain, rushing him. Limbs twist, organs bloat. Skin stretches and fire dances beneath.

Stay. Stay in the valley.

Drip.

Drip.

Drip goes the morphine.

On hind legs, Hoofy stands tall. Ears rotate. Blood pumps. The large red stone bangs inside his chest, rattles his ribcage.

Who goes there?

The slow rub of an animal in the grass.

Friend or foe?

Hoofy's nostrils flare. Greens bruise and release chlorophyll to the honey-hinted morning. Calendula—a larger paw than his crushed that amber flower. A new smell blooms, masked so long by pond odour, an undertone of rot, a fair trace of old blood: the ground reverberates with footfalls.

The tomcat.

Hoofy thumps the warm earth.

Danger.

The tom is rust and cream with a torn ear lending menace to his thick, whiskered cat face. He is street-wizened, long-clawed, and decorated in scars that slash his dirty fur. A hunter: languid and intoxicating. Each feline step echoes with a promise of violence that draws Hoofy, enchanted, as though on some level his body knows it must be offered up as in ancient rite.

He is prey. He prays.

All summer long Hoofy witnessed the tom's virility. Not just the swagger caused by obscene testicles protruding from hind legs. Valley nights echoed with the lowing, bleating yowls of heat. Females, crazed with need, escaped brick fortresses to drag their bellies through mud, asses raised, shameless. Night after night, until the wail of frenzied song became lodged in Hoofy's own soft muzzle, his shy and complicated head, his confused genitals. The tom's offspring—some pale as the tip of his tail, a butterscotch blend; others blatant orange and wide across the forehead like their father—get plucked by hawks or coyotes or sensitive ladies. Others are run off by their sire, who's as likely to maim them as he is Hoofy.

Hoofy leaps.

There: rust and cream, the iconic torn ear as the tom turns his head. Hoofy and he regard one another like lovers in this millisecond that stretches longer than night. Then Hoofy darts, a brown blur clearing a ringed tree stump, knocking the mushroom shelf in his haste, rounding the wild roses, thorn-tipped stalks ripping at his fur.

Hoofy leaps again.

The tom slinking closer, handsome beast, bloodthirsty with a belly full of worms.

Hoofy dives through ivy fall.

The tom pounces. Misses. Growl becomes scream, fur standing, tail fat with rage. The tom crouches, fangs bared.

A cold shadow passes: stainless-steel tools, white tile, chemical spray. Light searing his gauze-wrapped eyes. Voices again, and metallic beeping.

Hoofy cries out. The boy longs to be crushed by orange fur, cradled and delivered by merciful teeth. The hare fights to live.

"Shit," says Carole.

Norm activates the alarm: code blue.

"Jesus," he says. Sets his mug on the side table, misses, it clatters to the floor, bounces, the lid flies off and his pantlegs get soaked. Coffee, everywhere.

Norm runs for the defibrillator.

Carole compresses Hoofy's stripped chest, tight fist covered by flat palm, her nails bared. Says, "Come on, come on, Hoofy!"

She breathes, she counts, she thumps his solar plexus.

Breathe, count, thump.

She wills the red stone to ignite.

Pristine

ONE WEEK ON, five off, that's the routine, but the schedule is posted and Harper's got me back on decontam.

Over my shoulder Lucinda says, "Harper hates your guts, Mare."

"But I'm so charming. Why are you always on clean?"

Lucinda smiles. God, she's a looker.

"Not that I blame the guy."

I turn toward her. "You sure he can meet all your needs?"

Lucinda laughs and it's reckless, deep. Her head knocks back. She's wearing perfume despite the scent-free policy, and I breathe coconut, a hint of jasmine. I take hold of her wrist—its underside is pure sateen—and pretend to look at her watch. "We got time." My fingers itch to trace the length of her forearm. To cup her elbow and draw her whole body closer, to feel the heat rolling off it.

She quits laughing. Cocks a perfectly arched eyebrow. She's curious, but would she really take the plunge with an old butch like me?

"See you on the other side," she says, and those sweet hips shimmy the corridor.

Scrubs never looked so good. Lucinda is all abundance under that green cotton, no doubt.

"Suit up, *Mary Louise*," says Harper as he rounds the corner, nostrils flaring.

He really does hate me.

Tall, gangly, thick glasses, fringe around his dome top. Pot belly nudging his shirt front. Lucinda could do way better. Must like his money. What else could it be? He's clicking his pen, clipboard in the other hand. Nervous. Probably heard Lucinda's sexy laugh.

"Morning, Boss," I say.

Harper, you fucking piece of shit.

My mantra penetrates him telepathically, we both know it, but what can he do?

Weeks ago at the staff Christmas party, Harper the idiot, drunk on spiked eggnog, dangled mistletoe over Lucinda's flushed cleavage. Rumour has it she's been riding him ever since.

I smile and cross my arms.

Splotches migrate north of his collar. Harper jingles keys like he's in a big hurry and unlocks his office door. Probably updating his Christian Mingle profile or screwing up another crossword. When he ducks inside that beige oasis, puts a solid door between us, his whole body softens. He's safe.

I strut down the hall. *Two for two.*

SOW is a cornucopia of titties and sagging ass. Night shift's ending, morning's gearing up: double the pong in the women's locker room. It's too early for so much bush on only one coffee. Lockers creak open, get kicked shut. That joke of a shower trickles cold and someone shrieks. Automatic dryers crank, nozzles are twisted up to dry hair and armpits.

Inside my locker it's the same sad story. Uniform folded on the top shelf. Steel-toed boots lined up on the bottom.

Ancient photo of me and Shirl—fifteen years ago when we first hooked up—still taped to the door. Broads around here think she's my sister. God we look young: arms around each other, faces pressed close. My throat heats up. You think you know someone. You think things are just different now, that you're *maturing* into your adult life; it's not the hellcat pent-up chaos of those early years. You're partly relieved. Thing is, you just didn't know a rekindling was possible—loinfire—for you or for some other lucky slob.

Off go my Dickies. I hang the belt loops on my locker hook. Unsnap my shirt, quick peek around, hang it on the opposite hook.

After she sat me down, Shirley cleared out her stuff pretty quick. Must have been thinking about what to take for a while. Left holes like shrapnel all through the living room, the bedroom, the kitchen cupboards. I'd long ago stopped thinking of things as belonging to her or to me; they were simply in the house, ours, together. But I had to saw open a can of soup for dinner the night she left, didn't I?

I'm down to tube socks, boxers, and a thick-ribbed beater. Typical loungewear for a night on the couch, me and my six-string and my buddy Jack Daniels.

I crumple the picture in my fist. Set it on the shelf.

"Quit staring, Bulldagger," says that crackpot Erma next to me, and I go, "You wish."

I got the V-neck top on, ID clip, drawstring pants. Step into and lace up my steel-toes. Blue, papery boot wraps are on, my archnemesis the goddamned hairnet is next. Armed with my precision-made stainless-steel comb, got to trap every bloody hair. Long, not a problem: tie it. Short or none, you're flying. You got a serious rock 'n roll pompadour situation, such as myself, you got trouble. Tuck it in, it feathers out the other side. Scoop the front curl under, your ducktail's out.

Forty minutes *minimum* to style it each morning. Then ten to twelve waiting, thirty on the bus all the way down to the hospital loading dock. Then three to five before I'm in SOW, stripping down, suiting up, my look already ruined. But. Those three to five crazy-making pre-shift minutes, that's when I get Lucinda *in the flesh*. That's fuel for a lot of lonely hours, strumming my guitar, crooning to the night.

If you seen Lucinda and you seen the way she sometimes looks at me, you'd wake up early and slick your pomade, too.

Otherwise, why bother getting up.

"Mare-Mare! Mary Louise! Me and you, decontam, right?"

Murray. Hollering through the cracked-open change-room door.

"Yeah," I shout, but there's interference.

Women scream, "Fuck on off out of here, jackass Murray, get back to BOAR." Erma winds up and pitches her deodorant. It shatters on the wall beside Murray's face.

"Ow, Erma," he says, and he leaves.

"Bad enough *you're* here," Erma mutters.

"You love it," I say.

Scrubs on, time to wash—up to the elbows, between the fingers, knuckles, hand backs, nails. Snap on the latex. Snap on a second pair. Pull on a half-mask, settle it on the nose and mouth, stretch and release the elastic straps behind the head. Stare into my bloodshot eyes in the mirror above the sink. Great look if you're a serial killer. Crow's feet. A stubborn crease in the brow, that's new. Twelve years on the job, time flies. Shirley was the one who pushed me. Wanted health benefits, stability, a pension. Liked those paycheques. Got a little too lonely with all my overtime, as it turns out.

The damn straps. That dull ache builds up the back of my skull all shift, creeps behind the eyes, until a path is blazing, a lightning bolt, a house on fire. Ten hours from now, when I'm returned to myself—signed out, hosed off, and back in street clothes—the pain will be dimmed by four tallboys, a couple Vicodin, and Lucinda's hot ghost. What else is there? Just need enough to knock me flat, so I can wake up and do it all over again.

And every morning: silence.

The empty bed.

It starts with shoving. Hands on shoulders. Two sets, Shirley's and mine, the night we met. No. No. Start over. Lucinda's and mine. A stumbling tango to the supply closet. Good. Inside, we knock into things, shit rolls off shelves, mop handles clatter the broomsticks. We are tit-on-tit, hot-crotched together, slamming against the porcelain sink, careening into the cupboard. Little sounds come from her, *uhn*. I let go of her shirt, pull her hair, expose her long neck and bite into it; the sweetest pulse between my teeth.

Double metal doors, double slam.

SOW is deserted. Just me and these going-nowhere thoughts. *Shit*. A lull while I locate my ID card, which is clipped to my shirt hem but tucked into the waist of my pants. Got to swipe it once, twice. It beeps clearance. That's me, late, probably get docked. Last thing I need, now I'm stuck paying the full rent. Automatic doors slide open. The windowless metal corridor is a rusted ramp heading to the basement. Echoes of those broads bounce around the tunnel ahead. Orthopaedic, hard-toe trudge, voices—nasal and shrill—always complaining. Under-eye pouches, acne. Extra weight on the torso, thick ankles, and loose skin at the neck: lifers. God, don't let that be me. Let me die in a ditch before I lose myself to this pit.

Another slam.

I pick up the pace, trot the last stretch, round the corner. Got to swipe again, got to retinal scan—secure wing, authorized personnel only. Pause before the click. Push with my bent elbow, push. Doors swing inward here, negative air pressure, a contained ventilation system. Tunnel wind sucks in around me, the magnet pull of this soiled room trapping our dirty air inside. Can't let it drift upstairs. Upstairs is for the rich and the diseased, for the insured elite.

Decontam is dark and fetid and everything smells a little too ripe. Like breathing through a pair of old pantyhose, through the stinked-out crotch gusset. Erma says it reminds her of swamps back home. I say it's like dyke night at the Bathhouse, and that shuts them up. Honestly, I haven't gone cruising since 2005. Once I hooked up with Shirley that was it, I barely looked around and never looked back. Kept my leather jacket but sold the motorbike: bad move. She used to love clinging to me, wind filling our mouths, engine rattling our bones, when we roared out of the city. Made our escape to the southern blip of the fishing town that spat me up: swimming in the murky lake, bonfires on the beach, fucking in the green tent we got half price at Canadian Tire.

How am I to start fresh?

All the dykes I know have kids.

All our bars have been shut down.

If there still *was* a club, I'd take Lucinda. Hand on the curve of her back. Steer her to a barstool, park it. Buy her a drink, something with fruit. Whisper in her ear, give her the lowdown. Point out the lughead butches drooling in the corner, the uptown, slacks-wearing phonies. Treat her real good. Smile. *Listen*. Shirley said I never listen; totally not true. Shirley could even *be* there with her new twink, the one she met on the computer. The computer I bought her for Christmas two years ago. The damned thing. I'd slip my arm around

Lucinda's waist and make her giggle. Shirley'd lose her shit. And I know my way around a dance floor. I'd take Lucinda, a real cheesy number, and pull her close. Feel her breath catch when I dip and twirl her.

"Mare-Mare! Mary Louise!"

Fucking Murray.

"You're late. You seen the game last night?" he says.

"Yeah."

"You seen the overtime? Good goal, eh?"

"Yeah," I say. "Good goal."

Murray's an old dog, one you don't want anymore but can't bring yourself to put down. Shirley never could abide him. Didn't want him in the house. And I thought it was because she didn't like men.

I grab the closest wheeled cart. It's taller than me, heavy as hell. Do a U-ey, roll to the double sinks, big fuckers back-to-back all down the middle of the room. Forty trays per cart, nine carts, total. Trays are a mix—ortho, C.V., lapro—all plastic-wrapped. Gynie's are the worst, I leave them for last. Slide out the trays, unwrap the plastic, pick them clean. All these barbaric instruments have actually been *inside* some other person, cutting out their worst parts. Their cancers and ulcers and abscesses; their hairy, pus-filled fibroids. Their too-big or too-small tits, their crooked noses. Ah, the pretty people.

Sort the heavy tools first—hammers, bone saws, drills, then scalpels. So much for point-of-use prep, lazy fucks upstairs always leave biohazards. Gotta shake off the gore—yellowed fat, bone chips, fluids already corroding the finish. Lay the tools in the bins. Set the full bins on the conveyor belt. Then the smaller implants; the trokers, insufflators, pairs of pins—gotta wonder when there's only one. Next, paper and plastics: feed tubes, IV scraps, all the wrappers, crumpled pick sheets, sponges. Whatever's on the tray, it's got to go someplace.

It's not rocket science. In fact, it's boring as hell. Three of us unload and sort. Rumour is they're going to automate, and we'll all be out of a job. Pray for a good settlement. For now, we work. Got to put Murray by the tunnel washer because he sings so loud. Bloody awful, loves the Bee Gees. *How deep is your love?!*

I pull with the left hand, peel with the right. Shake shake rinse, chuck in the bins. Shake shake rinse, chuck in the bins. Then, pull with the left hand, peel with the right. Easy enough, but after an hour my rotator cuff starts burning and I'll never make it through shift.

I pull the sodden mask. "Murray!"

"Yeah?" Murray's cap is puffed like he got a rack of curlers from the corner salon. Scabby eczema flakes cling to his shoulders, chest, round belly. He's never on clean. Pigeon-toed, knees permanently bent, walking on the balls of his feet, he carries a bin.

"Got any of your mom's pills, Buddy?" I lick my lips.

"Might," he says.

"Give me one?"

"For ten dollars," he says.

"Thought we were friends."

"Yeah," he says, laughing. "But you owe me money."

"Huh. That so?"

"Yeah. You owe me sixty dollars, remember?"

I say, "Oh, shit. How 'bout we grab a beer after work, you and me?"

"Okay, Mare-Mare. Okay, Mary Louise. Let's grab a beer. Let's watch the game."

"Pay you then. Wallet's in my locker," I say, patting my scrubs.

Murray's eyes shrink. That guy loves his coin. Erma shoots a mean look, but there's no way she can hear us, not over the machinery.

I say, "Who's your buddy?"

"You are."

Murray reaches into his pants pocket, pulls out a baggie.

"Whoa, not here, Murray. What are you, stupid? Okay, slide me one now and one for later."

Swallow it dry.

I drive to Lucinda's place at the end of the night. Can't take her to mine. She'd take one look at that wasteland and see me for what I really am—a derelict bachelor with no can opener. She'd scram. Start again. Back to the bar. Walk her down to the lake. Maybe in spring, before the sewage-reeking heat waves and after the long icy winter. Walk her down to the lake under a full moon. Ask her things, get her talking, *fucking listen*. Make a joke—not too dirty. Don't say anything controversial; no politics, don't argue, just let this night ride the surface of good manners and charm. Look into her eyes. Invent a better version of yourself: the lure, the hook; the long, slow reel. The promise of all that sex. Then the relaxing back into your real selves, waiting for it to end.

This last part can go on for years.

Once the belt is full of bins, me and Murray drag the heavy plastic sheeting all the way around in its tracking. Some industrial shower curtains, more like shutters. We get a breather. Masks off, latex balled up and pitched. There are two chairs and one wobbly stool for sitting. I'm humming, smiling. Feeling pretty good, all things considered

When she started hitting the gym, that's when I should've known. Spin class and power yoga and gone, gone, all the soft familiar folds from her belly. No more canoodling on the couch eating potato chips. Shirley was looking real good.

Not like herself. Like a cleaned-up stranger, hungering.

I hit the switch. Cycle on. Hot rinse. More steam, that's all my hair needs. So humid the air has substance, filling my mouth. The buzzer sounds. Sanitizer liquid explodes into the wash. Cumulous clouds of disinfecting suds tower, topple, manifest again. Inside the plastic it's heaven minus god. The deafening buzzer. Repeat, rinse, then dry. Cover my eyes. A chemical wind billows two hundred and fifty, sixty, seventy degrees Fahrenheit, rattling the protective sheets. A tornado, a desert storm. Killing the parasitic, the bacterial, the viral. Wind drops, motor unwinds to a tick. We're battered. Got to collect our precious shards, assess the damage.

I stagger over to pull the lever. Conveyor belt grinds into gear, metal undulates. Everything pitches and tremors, thundering seismic from the tunnel washer, dividing us from them. Just that small square opening in the wall. Now our muck is purified, rolling, pristine, to the other side.

Daughter of Cups

"YOU KNOW what to do," he says. "Pretty girl like you."

It's like a baby eel in her hand, skin as smooth but hot, dry. Ohio lets go and it bounces against his beer belly. She laughs.

Don takes hold of her wrist. "Like this," he says, pressing. His *Live to Ride* belt buckle jingles when her hand pumps. He breathes louder through his nose, a high-pitched whinny on the exhale. Ohio wants to give him a Kleenex but she doesn't have one. She stares at the tattoos covering his forearms and biceps and peeking out the sleeves of his black T-shirt. Don's face is tan and wrinkled, his stubble silver. His eyes crinkle shut.

Ohio closes hers, too. The curl and crush of waves smacking the sandy shore lulls her. Now she is Melanie Williams—blonde, popular, stacked—and Don is Kevin Moody, the cutest boy at school.

After, Don drives off and leaves her sitting at the end of the Lake Erie pier. She squints across to Sandusky. She can swim, but how far? She can dive, sink to the weedy muck and disintegrate surrounded by treasure and ballast from long-ago shipwrecks, succumb to the naiads, handmaids to the lake queen, as per campfire lore when she was a kid. Or she can walk back to town, north on the main road. Ohio hoists herself up and walks. She can keep going to the highway and hitch the hell out of here, or she can turn left at the only stoplight. She stands in the heart of town, eying the fingernail sliver of moon in the still-bright summer sky.

Eeny meany miney moe.

Friday night. The bank clock says eight-thirty. A car drives by and Darryl Hicks chucks a crushed beer can out the window.

Ohio turns left, toward home.

At the convenience store she scours magazines until Mr. Cooper yells, "Gotta be eighteen!" She buys Fun Dip. There's a crisp twenty-dollar bill in her pocket, but she doesn't break it, not for candy. Across the street the Bingo is packed—cars zigzag on the grass and sidewalk. She jumps on the gas station hose to ring the service bell, so Tommy Knight will have to get off his lazy ass. She keeps walking. The closer she gets, the stronger it smells: dirty chicken grease blowing from the KFC. The Colonel's secret spice is her homing device. She sits on the KFC stoop. Stares at the empty road, eats Fun Dip. Dips the candy stick into the grape powder and licks. Dips and licks.

Her mom yells out the upstairs apartment window, "Ohio, where you been?"

"Nowhere!"

The window slams shut.

Ohio waits for something to fall from the sky.

Don had said, "What kind of name is that, anyway?"

He'd gotten it wrong, twice.

"That's me," she'd said, pointing over the lake.

"Erie?"

"Ohio."

"Wiyot—I knew a girl called that," he said.

"Not Wiyot. *Ohio*. Like the state."

"Some kind of Indian name?"

"That's where my mom had me."

"Oh," he'd said. "Used to work the car plant over in Sandusky. Good union job. 'Til I got jumped in with the boys."

Full truth: she was named Ohio because that's where her mom met the man and fell in love and that's where her mom got knocked up and where she gave birth, on the side of the road, right where the man left her. Her mom says they're never going back. Says she hid her baby girl up in her sweater and brought her across Lake Erie in a bartered boat. Swears a monster, the fabled queen of the lake, emerged from the depths, demanding a toll. No word of a lie. In exchange for safe passage, her mother sheared the matted ropes of her hair with a knife, dropped them overboard with her maidenhead, sacrificing her womanly powers. The waters quieted, and she paddled all the way back to her hometown. Been here ever since.

"Whatcha doin'?"

It's Mary Louise, who lives in a run-down bungalow on the other side of the KFC. She pushes her glasses up her nose. A piece of tape holds the broken arm in place. Mary Louise's mom cuts her hair using a mixing bowl as guide, which makes her look like a medieval clown. Mary Louise is twelve, two grades behind Ohio. Her parents regularly kick her out so they can party all night.

"Oh-*hi*-Oh," she says, "Can I have some?"

Ohio gives her the last bit of powder. Mary Louise jams her finger in the corners of the packet and sucks back and forth until it's gone. Her mouth and finger are purple. Ohio wipes her face hard on her sleeve.

Motorcycles.

The girls lean forward at the first faraway rumble. Reverberating bass fattens with grinding gears that choke and pop, that spit like gunfire. Sky begins to shake. Like a funnel cloud ripping from the west, gathering strength, flattening an unrepentant path in its wake, the hogs' engines detonate a primal roar in Ohio's cranium: her mouth waters, belly pools to nausea. A red sun hangs low in the sky; its light explodes off chrome, blinding. Motorcycles fill the road, two across. Ohio shields her eyes with sugar-stained fingers. Her molars vibrate, her braids dance. Ribs rattle, thighs too. The girlfriends sit tight behind the men, long hair slapping vests as they zoom past. There's darkness in the leather. Boots clamp silver stirrups.

Ohio can't breathe; her mouth is full of metal, her nose of gasoline.

Mary Louise claps like a headcase. "Two, four, six, nine—thirteen!"

Don, the last biker, rides alone. As he passes, Don winks and pops a wheelie.

Ohio sits taller on the stoop. A secret flush dapples her skin, heats the bill in her back pocket. Earlier that afternoon, Don had thrust forward with a gurgled shout, releasing himself in long arcs on the sand. One gush had landed wet on her leg and dried like snot. He'd zipped himself, smaller and softer, back into his jeans. *That's a good girl.*

Mary Louise looks at Ohio, mouth open.

An engine backfires somewhere down the road.

"You *know* him?"

Ohio shrugs. Why didn't he stop, put her on the back? Take her away from this place?

Later, Mary Louise says, "Why don't they ride their own bikes?"

"Who?"

Ohio is shrinking. Pieces of her dull life fall back into place now that Don and the bikes have vanished.

"The girls."

"Those things are really heavy, Dork."

"I guess."

If Ohio's mom had had her own motorcycle, maybe she wouldn't have been such a mess when the man dumped her ass. Might have fixed him good, stone-pillar punishment. Wouldn't have severed her own Goddess head and dumped it in the lake, defeated. When she was a kid, Ohio had a green two-wheeler she pedalled everywhere—banana seat and tall, rusted handles with streamers like seaweed. That was joy, the kind of freedom she'd never have traded.

"Even my dad can't fix his," says Mary Louise, hopping from one foot to the other. "It's been in pieces all over the garage since I was born."

Ohio climbs on top of the KFC garbage can. Says, "Your dad's a dick. No offense."

"It's getting dark," says Mary Louise. "I'm going home."

"Move it, Ohio."

Saturday morning.

Ohio sprawls on the bed. Her mom pulls the faded seahorse-print sheets out from under her, spilling Ohio this way and that as she yanks them off the mattress. Her mom's stubby ponytail shivers with every tug. Her hair is greasy and there are dandruff flecks near the roots. She stuffs the sheets into a basket of dirty clothes.

Ohio flattens face down, arms and legs a starfish. "I never get to do anything," she says into the mattress.

"You get to do the laundry any minute."

"No!" Ohio curls like a sea urchin and transports herself to Atlantis. She's a mossy-haired beast with venom-tipped fangs.

Her mom sits on the edge of the bed, and her weight sags the mattress. Ohio rolls into her, unbidden. Her mom wears stretch pants, a too-tight Club Med T-shirt, and the pink-sparkle flip-flops Ohio gave her for Christmas. The waistband at the back of her pants is frayed. Ohio can see the large mole a couple inches above her crack through the thin, grey fabric.

"Ohio."

Ohio grunts.

"I'm doing the groceries."

"You're changing, right?" says Ohio.

"What's your problem?"

Ohio chokes on the memory of her mom wearing these same pants while bending into other people's trash for empties, to get the deposit.

Waste not. Want not.

Ohio says, "I hate this town."

Her mom sighs and her shoulders droop.

"It's not the worst place in the world."

She heaves off the bed and the mattress plumps back up. Sets the laundry basket on an old skateboard they found at the beach and rolls the towering pile to the door. Ohio is supposed to push it all the way through town like that.

"No wonder I don't have a boyfriend," says Ohio.

"Oh, you *think* you want a man," says her mother. "Divide your money and multiply your sorrow. I was a bit older than you when I started working summers at the factory."

"Right."

"I was bored, so I quit."

"I get it."

"Had some adventure. Met your smooth-talking snake of a father. Haven't been bored since."

"*You're* the one who liked him," says Ohio.

"Loved." She hands over some quarters and the box of detergent. "I'm on afternoons. Be home late."

Ohio kicks open the door and lets it slam behind her. Mary Louise is curled in the stairwell. "Morning, Oh-*hi*-oh!" Her hair sprongs in all directions and she's got the same shirt on as yesterday, only dirtier.

"You can't go downtown like that," says Ohio, and goes back inside to grab a clean shirt from her dresser. She tosses it to Mary Louise and slams the door again.

"Put yours in the basket."

"Okay."

Ohio hauls the basket down the steps. Mary Louise gets the skateboard. They push the laundry up to the stoplight. It's hard work, even with both of them. South one block to the Coin-o-Matic. Penny Middleton's sister is inside with two dirty kids. One of them doesn't even have pants on, just a filthy T-shirt and bare bum, tiny bobbing penis. Penny Middleton's sister's big belly pushes out from her T-shirt and joggers. The hard knot of her bellybutton stares: kid number three! Ohio picks the farthest away washer and loads it, measures out soap. Mary Louise jams in the quarters. The machine shudders. Water spits onto the clothes and the girls can't help it, they thrust their hands inside to cup the rush, let it soak their thirsty skin. When the machine is filled, Ohio slams the lid. It's hot, so they sit outside on the plastic chairs.

Kevin Moody walks by with his peach-fuzz moustache and his blond hair parted down the middle, a perfect flip on each side. His tight jeans are ripped at one knee and bunched at his puffy white sneakers.

Ohio tosses her braids and wishes they were blonde. She puckers up, as if readying for a kiss. She read all about how to get your lips noticed in *Teen Beat Magazine*. Kevin Moody stands in front of her, obviously noticing her lips.

He says, "Is that your sister?"

Ohio turns. Mary Louise has one finger up her nose.

"What is she, retarded?"

"Fart off," says Mary Louise. She flicks a goober at him.

"You girls are the ugliest chicks in town, you know that?" Kevin shakes his head and keeps walking.

"After your mama," shouts Mary Louise.

Ohio slugs Mary Louise on the arm, hard. "No one picks their nose in front of Kevin Moody."

"Who cares," says Mary Louise. "He's a burnout."

Saturday night, TV is broken. Melanie Wilson, also going into grade nine, is having a party, but Ohio isn't invited. Lying on the linoleum, she fingers the Great Lakes on the most worn page of their atlas. Voices like tiny cracked bells whisper: *join us*. There's an X pencilled north of Put-In-Bay, where her mother saw the beast. A zigzag line traces their journey along the chain of cormorant- and gull-infested islands—Rattlesnake, Sugar, the Sisters—where they stopped to rest. It took days. The crap motor conked out and her mom had to row. "This is how you got here," she says, showing her biceps. And, "You're lucky to grow up in Canada. We got health care." Another X on Pelee Island, where a local took pity and drove them to the ferry dock. Ohio was just a newborn, but sometimes memories surge: the slosh of waves against a rusty bow, the thud and creak of oars in the outriggers, the smell of fish and gasoline, and the fearsome sound of her mother by turns swearing, weeping, beseeching the gods, all the way across the lake. "All for you," her mother likes to say.

In the atlas, Ohio finger-trails a shoal of minnows against the current, leaves Lake Erie, enters Lake Ontario, floats down the adjoining canal. Watersogged, she beaches on the Manhattan shore. With her eyes closed, she can be anyone. A runaway in New York City. A waitress. A drug lord boss baby.

Madonna sings *Papa Don't Preach* on the kitchen radio and Ohio gets up to prance in the kitchen. She's all slippery legs and dark eyes; an empty belly, hands open, begging.

At the back of the freezer, hidden behind the fish sticks, is a small bottle of vodka. Ohio takes a swig. It burns her throat. The heat fades to a warm glow. She gulps again. She puts on her mom's make-up using the kitchen mirror: coral lips, sea-foam lids, tangled green lashes. Ohio's thick hair is natty, coiled with life, like her mom's used to be. She has her mother's eyes—stony black, damning—but her skin is darker, more like the man's.

Ohio undoes her buttoned shirt and ties it above her waist. She's as flat as the Erie pier, but it looks good with tight shorts. Especially when she puts on her mom's cork-heeled sandals. She peels the forbidden leather vest off the final hanger at the back of her mom's closet. It smells like mildew and stale tobacco, like something wild and not quite dead in a ditch. Its weight is armor across her shoulders. It gapes under the arms, in the chest, where her mom's notorious rack stretched it out, once upon a time, that summer she ran with the gang.

"You look like a hooker."

"Thanks."

Mary Louise turns down the music and sits on a stool at the kitchen counter. "You left the door open. I could hear the radio outside."

"So?"

"So, you're lucky it's only *me* who came up."

"Am I ever."

Ohio pouts and blots her lips with toilet paper. Pieces of it cling to the lipstick. She swaggers to the freezer, pulls again from the bottle.

Mary Louise pushes her glasses up her nose. "Alcoholic," she says, blinking.

"As if."

"You're gonna do this all night? Boring."

Ohio says, "You're right. Let's go downtown."

It takes longer walking in the shoes. As she goes uphill, Ohio's feet slide backwards with each step. She tries to buy smokes at the convenience store. Mr. Cooper says, "Nice try, Ohio. Mom working tonight?"

Mary Louise steals Pop Rocks and they sit in the parking lot, letting the tiny pink crumbs explode in their mouths: stinging sugar pings. Bingo is rammed, cars everywhere, motorized wheelchairs parked in a crooked line down the block.

"Look." Mary Louise points to the gas station. It's Don filling his Harley. She waves wildly until he nods back.

"Come on," she says, trotting over.

Ohio follows, nearly wiping out on the curb.

"Ladies," he says, staring at Ohio.

Ohio cringes, tugs the vest. Should she button it or leave it loose to show her bellyskin? Her mom wore it over a studded bra the summer she was seventeen, waitressing the biker bar in Ohio. That and a pair of cut-offs showing the smiles of her ass. Says they queened her, over in America. Says she made great tips, mostly. Then she met the man.

Don's eyes peel away the make-up, the shorts, the slutty shoes. They linger on the leather, on a silver pin above her right nipple—entwined adders, tongues flicking one another.

He says, "Where'd you get that?"

"Yard sale," she lies.

"You're flagging colours, Sweetheart."

Don opens her vest, fiddles with the pin and removes the backing, pulls it free from the leather. He reattaches the backing and tucks the pin into the tiny vest pocket with a fat finger. "Gang stuff. Never wear what you don't know," he says.

"My dad has a motorcycle but it's broke," says Mary Louise. She points to Don's large belt buckle. "R-ride to live—"

"Live to ride," he finishes. "Know what that means?"

She shakes her head, no.

"Means there's nothing better on this earth. Wanna?"

Don sets his helmet on Mary Louise's head and carefully tightens the strap. Ohio is stabbed by a jealous fork, seeing the way Don tucks strands of flyaway hair into the helmet. He lifts and settles Mary Louise in front. Last time he gave her a ride, Don helped Ohio onto the wide leather seat, but today she scrambles up on her own. She wears the girlfriend helmet. The motorcycle leans to one side when Don kicks the stand away and the muffler burns Ohio above her ankle. She clenches her mom's shoes at an angle so she won't get burned again.

Don revs the engine. Mary Louise squeals. Ohio is pancaked on his back just like the biker girls. Don smells like gasoline, sweat, and cigarettes. He says something Ohio can't hear, not with the helmet on, not with the hot motor running between her legs, vibrating everything.

They hit the street with a lurch. Wind rushes Ohio's face. Aphids swarm her open mouth like tiny fish. They turn south at the stoplight and she's sure she'll fall, but she doesn't. They cruise past the Coin-o-Matic, they're coming up to the Legion, the only bar, where a bunch of kids are smoking out front. Don opens her up, gets the lead out, and they speed the rest of the way to the pier.

Take that, Ohio thinks, squeezing tightly.

At the lake, Don turns off the motor and kicks the stand. He lifts Mary Louise and sets her down, takes the helmet off her head. Her lunatic grin is contagious.

"Live to ride, ride to live," she chants.

Don doesn't offer to help Ohio, so she slides off the leather seat, puts her weight onto one wobbly shoe, and lifts her other leg over the back of the bike. She sets it, trembling, onto the ground. She removes the helmet and shakes her braids. Don and Ohio walk across the sand and sit on a large, flat rock. Mary Louise twirls around, sugar high, leaps to the water's edge. She skips flat stones, throws driftwood spears at waves, draws in the sand with a stick.

The red glow of the setting sun lights up one side of the lake like a fairy tale. The rest of the sky begins to darken. Ohio wonders what a real girlfriend would say. Don lights a home-rolled cigarette. He inhales, holds it in, slowly exhales. Stinky blue smoke hangs in the air. He passes it, and she copies him. It pinches her throat worse than the vodka. Makes her choke. Is she smoking pot?

"Why'd you dress like that?"

"Dunno." Ohio looks down at the skin folds bunching on her stomach. She sits up and they disappear.

"How old are you, sixteen? Seventeen?"

Ohio takes another puff so she doesn't have to lie, or worse, tell the truth. She'll be fifteen next spring. Her mouth is dry. She reaches under the vest and unties her shirt, smoothing the fabric. She does up the buttons. After Don flicks the dead butt away, he puts his oil-stained hand on Ohio's thigh. He has a silver serpent ring and hairy knuckles. Ohio's heart beats so fast she might barf. Thoughts stutter in her mind: *Will I ever get boobs? Did I say that out loud? Did I already think that?*

"Get your friend," he says, pointing to the crest of a large wave.

Ohio hops off the rock. She runs, leaps. Her body feels strong; her arms slice through time and space, windmilling the warm air. She laughs. Slaps bare feet on wet sand, then into the cold lake. Water rushes her toes, freezes her ankles and higher up her calves, splashes her thighs. Shadows twist and reach from inside the curled wave. Somewhere in that murk a clam-crowned princess is living a life meant for Ohio, magic and free. Hair tangled and billowing with tide, skin pale and tantalizing as a trout belly, arms undulating hypnotically. Ohio dreams her almost every night: that tinkling ghost wail and the beckoning fingertips. Mary Louise flops closer and clasps Ohio's hand. They jump whitecaps, leaning their bodies to take the hit. Ohio knows there are no cowards underwater, only the softened, gnawed-upon bones of sailors, fishermen, and rum runners, cradled in ritual piles in the lake's darkest, coldest crook.

Under the surface all men want.

Under the surface all men love.

Don slides one hand around Ohio, the other around Mary Louise. An old man with two dripping girls shivering on a rock. "Let's show her what we did the other night." Don works the hand that had been on Ohio's leg inside her wet shorts, into the crotch.

That's not what we did, thinks Ohio.

Don's fingers push her goose-fleshed thighs apart. They press and flick a lightning rush of heat.

"Uh," she says.

Someone is walking a dog down the beach, so far away the dog is a leaping smudge on the horizon, the person a short stick.

"Don't worry, they can't see us," he says.

Ohio feels good, like something might happen next.

Don's other hand is busy with Mary Louise. Mary Louise leans forward. "Bor-ring."

Don says, "We do other things, too." Don pulls his hand from Ohio's shorts. His left hand resurfaces and rests on Mary Louise's leg.

"Like what?" says Mary Louise.

Don smiles at Mary Louise until she tilts her head and really sees him, until she starts smiling, too.

Ohio's tingling crotch spot is forgotten. Tossed over the gunwales with fish guts, net trash. Upstaged by a twelve-year-old with a crappy haircut. Ohio rubs off her lipstick with the collar of her shirt, smearing the cotton pink. "I'll show her."

Don turns back to Ohio. Her skinny legs swing from the knee, feet wet with grit. She wriggles her toes.

"Look at you," he says.

Ohio tugs on the buckle of his thick belt. When she stands she feels woozy, so she leans against the rock. She rubs him the way he showed her. Mary Louise quietly slides down and runs back to the water. Don frowns. They watch Mary Louise jump into foamy waves that purr onto the hard-packed sand.

"She okay out there?" he says.

"Of course. This is *our* lake." Ohio squeezes until Don faces her again.

"Careful," he says.

This time Ohio keeps her eyes open. Three stubbled chins bob in time with her hand. She can see right up Don's wide nostrils, see the grey hairs inside. His breath comes in hot blasts. White fluid shoots into her fist, drips from her fingers.

"Taste it," he says.

It is sea salty, the runny part of an undercooked egg, and when she swallows, the acid trails her throat.

"Like it?" he says.

Ohio falters, smiles.

"That's a good girl."

Don gives himself an extra shake and zips up. He lights a smoke and leans on the rock. A mosquito bites Ohio's temple. She swats, scratches, and a drop from her hand gets in her eye, stinging. She rubs it, making it worse. Don says something about a club meeting, says he'll see her around soon, he hopes. He leaves a crisp twenty-dollar bill on the rock beside her, "For a little treat, for you girls," and walks toward his bike.

Ohio's eye burns and waters. She slips the bill into her pocket.

The further Don gets on the darkening beach, the less Ohio sees. His head is a blur. His clothes blend with the night. A few more strides and he disappears.

Mary Louise jogs up from the water's edge. "Now you see him, now you don't. Like his thing." She cracks up.

Ohio says, "That's not funny." But it is, and she laughs, too.

Mary Louise yanks Ohio's arm. "His Thing," she shouts.

Ohio stumbles, tugs Mary Louise back, spinning her in the sand.

They shriek, "Thing Thing Thing!"

They spin like fireflies, whipping each other in circles until they collapse in a gritty pile, panting, hysterical.

Don's engine turns over once, twice; it roars. His headlight clefts the beach and lights up a circle of churning water.

"Look!" says Mary Louise, pointing.

"What? Where?"

Ohio hears it first: a tidal suck, the shrieking gale, the whizz and pop of meteorites. The hissing of a thousand jagged voices. Finally, Ohio sees her in the bike's spotlight—the legendary lake mother, bare-breasted with weedy swirls of hair. Suckling fish cloak her in open-mouthed kisses, flit at the swell of her barnacle-spackled hips. She dives. Dorsal fin splashes. A shimmering ripple—an iridescent web binding her legs, slick captives in silver scales. Here, the levy queen: she who exacts a toll for safe crossing. She who lures the friendless and the forsaken.

"Take him," says Ohio.

Ohio could feed him limb by limb to the surf; Mary Louise would help. Together, they can do anything. But Don's headlamp is already cutting an arc, lighting the pier, pointing toward the road. The dark settles. Just the motor whining quieter and the red brake light growing smaller, smaller.

Adoro Te Devote

THINGS that depress the hell out of me: stripped bicycles, their rusted parts still locked to the post; empty refrigerators; really old people eating alone.

The Smiths moaning on my Walkman, my five-foot-eleven reflection insulting the front hall mirror. String-bean, acne-ridden, beak-nosed. Sunken chest, pigeon-toed. This—my embarrassing teenage body—now added to the list of things that depress the hell out of me. Behind me, the pantry. Dinted cans of soup and tuna huddle beside a fleet of Heinz ketchup, purchased by the case at deep discount. Da demands ketchup, the greatest North American invention, at every meal. He loves bargains, but is enraged by the neon reduced-to-clear stickers.

"The whole town already knows what you make at the mill," says Mother. "You're not fooling anyone."

We're poorer than lots of kids at school but richer than some. Marie Belanger, whose dad is the mayor, is at the top of the money pile and Greggor Neilson, who owns every inch of my flesh, the boy who knows my Soul, is at the bottom. Father Casey says the poor and the meek shall inherit the earth, which I used to believe, but now I know the truth. Ask Morrissey—we'll be getting shit-all!

Da: tobacco and rye whisky and Irish Spring soap. Underneath that, the smell of sweat and physical labour, perseverance. He says Mother was a young fox when he and a cousin materialized in town, thinking they'd try seasonal farm work. A wiry Irishman, a sailor at heart, he struggled in the fields, so instead focused his efforts on the art of seduction. Flirty and dark-haired, he punched out a rival suitor, flattering her. Held the ladder like a gent when she climbed out her bedroom window. The elopement photo, taken the night of the harvest moon, shows them young and sparkly and hopeful, he with jaunty cap and uniform, she in a negligee and wool cape. Months later at the hospital, she cradles the bundle—me!—and he leans awkwardly into the frame. Soon after, he returned to sea and, for most of the 1970s, was a ghost who sent postcards from faraway lands, and whose sporadic visits began romantic and yielding, but usually ended in landlocked despair. I remember him shaking my little hand goodbye over the weeping that inevitably came from behind her closed bedroom door. After, I'd put on the kettle and go back to being Mother's *Little Man*, her only confidante.

I was eight when she bought the bungalow, using an inheritance from her mother. It took time to comprehend that this gift signified my stern grandmother's demise. Their elopement had humiliated her. Subsequently, she'd visited only once, the subject of many arguments. Every Sunday she sat near the front at Mass. I loved to hear her warbling soprano cut above the rest of the congregation. She was as old as some of the nuns, but glamorous: crinkly pale skin powdered with a circle of rouge on each cheek and a round, lipsticked mouth, clip-on pearl-drop earrings and a beaver collar fastened at her throat. Once a month she'd have us over after church and Mother and I would perch on antique chairs in the thickly carpeted sitting room watching reruns of *The Lawrence Welk Show*. We ate cucumber sandwiches with the crusts cut off and American cheese with pimento slices. The main event, tea, was properly poured by her housemaid, Sybil, and served with cubes of sugar in fine bone china. She was the closest thing to a movie star we had in our small town. At the end of each visit, Grandmother would sit at her desk in the study and painstakingly write out a cheque, sign and date it, and fold it in half, before presenting it to Mother. "For the boy," she always said. "Not a penny to that man."

Her relic-filled house was silent but for the ticking and chiming of an enormous grandfather clock, which, in some elaborate and deluded fantasy, I misconstrued as representing her husband, the grandfather I'd never met. After the funeral, Mother and I drove to the A&W, then idled in her driveway eating burgers out of their wrappers while Grandmother's estate was boxed and packed into two large trucks. "What will Grandmother do without her things?" I asked, and Mother replied, "what'll they do without her?" Most of the smaller stuff, the jewelry and furs and terribly delicate china, had been bequeathed to Sybil. When two unshaven men struggled to load the tall clock wrapped in bed sheets, I wept, half-mashed pickle and burger bun dropping from my mouth onto my pressed black trousers. I begged Mother to buy it and bring it home with us. She would not.

Despite my grief, Mother slapped a cheerful yellow on the bungalow's pantry walls. She papered the bedroom while I practiced words from the Oxford Dictionary. She loved that house, was sick of renting crap apartments from people in town, and for all I know she felt some sense of liberation now that her own mother had evaporated from our lives. The bungalow was nothing like Grandmother's Victorian mansion, but we were happy enough, the two of us baking pies and listening to Anne Murray on AM radio, dancing in our aprons while the oven glowed like the heart of a slumbering dragon.

Then came Da, to stay.

Mother called in a favour for his job at the mill and he gave up his mariner's life for good. He had to choose, she said. So did *she*, he said. And suddenly I was no longer her Little Man, her escort about town. I watched, indignant, as he fumbled, not even serving her tea the way she liked it. Tracking mud through the house. Flicking ashes from a chronic cigarette. Swearing, leaving the toilet seat up. The hopeful line on Mother's brow deepened, and things she once found charming now aggravated her. When I sang Barbra Streisand in the grocery store aisles, she shushed me. My Jane Fonda *Klute* impersonation, lip-puckering, hand-to-hip strutting through the parking lot, used to make her laugh. "You're too old for that, Pauly," she said in a tight voice. "People will think you're odd."

Da, when he returned for good, was restless and edgy. He worked and drank and sometimes fought. Weekends, he brooded in the house like a caged bear. Occasionally, my parents slow-danced on the lawn—a coarse, brown rectangle—shuffling clockwise around the roses. My chest constricted in those moments of betrayal, but when pressed Mother simply said, "Men have their needs, Pauly, what can I do?"

Da was angry but also sad, perhaps diseased, and that thing—whatever virus—hungered for vengeance, infecting our household. We became its victims and its hosts: hollowed out strangers, all three of us. Everything about me irritated him, so Mother took me up to Holy Mary's to see about becoming an altar boy. "It'll stop you getting underfoot," she said, and proceeded to make arrangements.

Things nobody knows: after Grandmother died, I smashed Mrs. Mastronardi's front window and blamed Greggor Neilson; I peed regularly on the rubber plant in the school foyer; I stole communion wafers from the rectory and at bedtime would place one on my tongue, letting it soften with the day's events, absolving myself of everything.

"God bless Father Casey and Holy Mary Immaculate Church of God, and the Pope in Rome. God bless Mother and Da, make them like each other," I'd say into clasped hands, "and God bless Sister Barbara, even if she is a toad." A few moments later, as I pulled on my small, tingling penis, I'd add, "God bless Greggor the brute and please, God, bless me."

In those years I imagined becoming a priest, just like Father Casey. Father Casey did not smell like other men. Not of cigarettes, whisky, sweat, and manure, or the chemicals used at the mill. I never saw him fill a gas tank or handle a power tool. He was old paper, dusty and clean at the same time, much like Grandmother's house, and that endeared him to me. His job was to sit and sip weak tea with a spot of milk, to eat endless pastries, to sample the homemade jellies of a hundred old ladies, and to listen. Comfort. Until the tea was drunk and all that remained of the little cakes were crumbs on the inevitable doilies. Mother did not normally bring food to the parish hall—"that's what nuns are for," she said—but she made efforts for church fundraisers. She always baked apple pie because Father Casey liked it best.

"What do I have to do to get a slice of that," Da would say. "Cut me dick off and wear a dress?"

The desperate day Mother approached Father Casey on my behalf, she spent all morning baking. I practiced genuflecting and signing the cross in the mirror. I fasted—something I'd heard other servers did before taking communion. Lastly, I tried on Mother's dressing gown, twirling to check the hem length, which approximated that of the requisite alb.

I would look very good as an altar boy.

We walked, me carrying the pie. It had a lattice top with cinnamon-sugar sprinkles, which I breathed rapturously. We entered the back door and tiptoed the dimly lit hallways, past the sacristy where the albs and cassocks and surplices for service hung. At his study door, she knocked and inquired after his health in her falsely optimistic voice. She reminded him I'd made first communion and had an affinity for the Church. "My Paul needs discipline, routine," she said, and rather unnecessarily added, "they don't like him at school."

An embarrassing understatement.

Recess, lunch, the twilight hours afterward, were armageddon. In dodge ball and Red Rover—boys, large and small, even the girls, even the whiney first years assaulted me. Their violence manifested in countless bloody noses, two chipped teeth, and thirteen stitches up the gullet from a hockey stick battering. My belongings were rigorously vandalized, most frequently with the words *Pauly is Fag-God.*

Father Casey may have looked at me with pity, but it was hard to tell; light reflected off his spectacles. Father Casey was stern and precise. He wanted his things laid out on the divan in the same order every day: white cotton undershirt and pants, socks, the alb, the cincture, and, most importantly the correct stole, depending on the liturgical season. Easy enough. His hands were large and old. Brown spots spread across the backs of them. White hair grew on his knuckles and crept out the ends of his shirt cuffs. He nodded at my red gingham snap shirt, my Lone Ranger belt buckle, and sassy red corduroys. "He'll need suitable clothes; dark pants and white shirt will do."

"Father, you're kind to help my Paul," she said. "He's an odd boy, but you have more patience than his Da, God bless you."

My apprenticeship was decided. Father Casey took a hard-boiled egg in the study, since he wasn't invited out to dinner, and I walked home with Mother.

Of all the altar boys, I alone would go to Holy Mary's after school each day, and wind my way to his private chambers. All my free time was spent in the quiet sacristy or the vestry, readying him for service. I had especially romanticized our entrance procession: me swinging the thurible, wafting incense, the other boys bearing lighted candles or carrying the cross. I loved to ring the altar bells during the recitation of the epiclesis, when Father Casey, like a magician, called down the Holy Spirit by extending his hands over the Gifts. Kneeling after the Agnus Dei, the ritual of the Mass and the ornate artistry of the Church mesmerized me. With Grandmother gone and her house boarded up, plundered by teen vandals, falling to waste—the sale halted due to some land transfer fiasco and, later, to crushing economic recession—this was the only beautiful place left.

Being a priest seemed like the one job I might be good at: listening, nodding, and repeating the magical Latin phrases in time with the spooky organ, just like Father Casey. I worshipped him, technically a sin, but Father Casey didn't mind. He always picked me to help with the Eucharist. I dreamed of apprenticing, of one day taking over. Becoming a priest meant I would not have to marry and beget children: tragedy averted. Most importantly, questions of sin—mortal versus venial, the works of the flesh versus the fruit of the

Spirit—preoccupied my young mind. I cherished each word from Father Casey's mouth.

I minded the schoolyard horrors less when I had the Church's mahogany walls; protective, velvet curtains; sculptures, and otherworldly paintings to transport me. My clothes and hair smelled of incense. My shoes were polished. Father Casey was gruff, predictable, but my role was clear. Of all Father's altar boys, I shone brightest.

Things I crave: radioactive romance; sparks and flames and a bonfire to singe the foliage from my pale branches, to burn and lay waste to this supernatural love of mine. I want small animals to flee in terror, birds to screech and reel in the blackened sky. I want a mattress soaked and torn. I want a city in ruins when I'm done.

Greggor Neilson was bred for a particular meanness that other children instantly recognize as authority. I love him, but it's complicated. At sixteen, Greggor is two inches taller and at least forty pounds heavier than me, all muscle. Thick-bodied and indestructible, a warning tick trembles in his sculpted cheek before he snaps. Even in kindergarten he was bigger than the rest of us, swearing like a trucker, sporting bruises and an older brother's Jethro Tull shirt.

In grade three, the public health nurse discovered lice in his hair and he was sent home. I was able to concentrate on learning in his absence, but the Greggor-less day was dull without his cruel attention. Greggor slunk outside the school fence and trailed me to Holy Mary's, chucking rocks. Father Casey let me go at twilight and Greggor tackled me in the bushes—the first of countless times. Pinned beneath him, I felt suffocated by the gamy smell of his unwashed clothes and sour breath.

"I seen you in the window," he said.

"What?" I said, in some kind of stupor.

"I seen you with the priest."

While I was in Father Casey's private chambers, setting out his things on the divan. Etcetera.

"I'm late for supper," I stammered.

Greggor rubbed his head furiously against my own, skull knocking skull. "Fuck yer supper, God Boy," he said through clenched teeth.

I ran, crying, conceivably to spread the dreaded nits at home. When I revealed the source of my dishevelment, Greggor's lice attack, Mother soaked my head in kerosene and Da spanked me for allowing it to happen. "Fight or flight, son, don't just stand there."

To this day I have no language for the things that transpire when one body collides with another, only a bewildering swamp of emotion. Yet I anticipate ambush in every form. As we creep toward repugnant adulthood, Greggor, so unlike me, so unashamed, remains my captor of choice, despite tempting me away from the Church. Father Casey, the nuns, my parents, all warn against him. But a depraved excitement races through me whenever he is near. I picture Greggor's strong, young body toppling Father Casey, the shining crucifix knocked from his grasp.

That boy.

Chest thumping in my shirt.

The world tilts, spins me senseless.

Grandmother's dilapidated house, allegedly haunted and a notorious, decade-old haven for drunkenness and fornication, is where I find him. Teenagers are routinely rounded up and sent home with warnings, forbidden to return, and Da gets calls to replace window boards after particularly raucous parties. I like to sit alone on the vandalized front porch, addressing her aloud just as I do Margaret

Thatcher and the Virgin Herself. "Beloved (Grand)Mother, Queen of Heaven, Undoer of Knots, who never refuses to come to the aid of a child in need." I list hardships and domestic grievances, beseeching her ghost to intervene on my behalf. *Judas Prist!* is newly carved across the derelict front door. A lump travels from throat to wretched guts. I'm glad she can't see the deplorable and misspelled state of things: fresh raccoon tracks from the caved-in roof, rusted hooks where once hung an early-twentieth-century porch swing. Poor old girl, I think. About Grandmother or the house, I'm not sure.

The first time I stumbled upon Greggor, I'd slipped behind the house and, after embarking on a monumental urination, noticed him halfway up a tree, smoking. His legs were stretched out on a thick branch, his back leaned against the barky trunk, *Hustler* magazine open in his lap, belt and fly undone. Most teenaged boys would be horrified, caught in the solitary act, but Greggor smoked his Du Maurier to the filter before stubbing it out on his jeans and flicking it. He jumped down into the clearing. Though desperate to leave, I could not interrupt the torrent of elimination.

"Horse piss, Fag God," he said.

And, "You stay, you play."

He dared me to do one thrilling thing after the other. Take off my shirt. Touch my bare chest. Look at the glossy pages he held in front of me—terrifying breasts, grotesque genitalia, and veiny, erect, sunglass-wearing men. He bade me copy the girls' poses, repeat dirty phrases out loud. He goaded, grunted, and I finally did each electric thing. After, he ziplocked the magazine in plastic, stuffed it inside the hole of a fallen tree and lit another smoke.

"See you around," he said, and I floated home to replay each sacred moment in my mind.

Wind shakes the leaves of a two-hundred-year-old oak. A goliath pine hides an eagles' nest that sheds poultry bones and fish tails and the collars of small dogs. A black iron fence demarcates the perimeter of our universe, the yard, pinecones underfoot. A corner with overgrown bracken is where we end up, no words exchanged, no notes passed, as though divine fate were driving us, not hormones. Sometimes he's not there, and I wait: hungry, anxious, alone. I'm at his mercy. From the first day we met at Holy Mary Immaculate, Greggor dominated; our sex is no different.

As foreplay, Greggor tells a raunchy joke or shoves his tattered *Hustler* at me or dispenses with all formality and simply throws me to the ground. This is totally normal for men, according to the *Cosmo* advice column I consume in the grocery store check-out line, causing Mother no small embarrassment. "Brooke Shields is hot stuff," I lie, waving the cover photo, but Mother's thin lips press together, her already pale face pinches grey with mortification.

"Pauly," she hisses, "put that down."

When I don't, she bumps me with the shopping cart, as if by accident. She swats me with a large box of Cornflakes.

Nevertheless, I shell out my dollar-ninety-five and absorb enough wisdom to learn that men have unbridled sex fantasies, it's in their nature, and if you do not fulfill them some other woman will. It behooves a girl to open her mind, to learn to anticipate such carnal leanings and meet them halfway. Wearing see-though panties is evidence of this commitment, for example. Even more important, once a man has been truly sexually satisfied, he will become tender and share intimate aspects of his otherwise impervious self. Greggor, after our most aggressive trysts, does in fact reveal glimpses of his home life—flashes of a tainted river running through him, dragging him under, filling his lungs.

"What's this?" I asked once, fingering the scars lacing his back.

"My old man's belt," he said, and promptly rolled over.

The idea that anyone could hurt Greggor astounds me. Nuns despise him but keep their distance, except for Sister Barbara, who grills him on unfinished homework in front of the class; more torture for me than him. Her withered skin slopes loosely from chin to the top of her blouse, that place where others have necks. I squeeze my fists under the desk and telepathically plant answers inside Greggor's head; but Greggor will not be saved. He slouches, eyes fixed on the tiled ceiling, looking like so many of the stained-glass saints in Holy Mary's hall, refusing to answer. Sister Barbara's deep voice quavers as she pronounces, "Neither heretics, nor homosexuals, nor sorcerers, nor liars, who shall all burn in the lake of eternal fire!" She wants us to know: Greggor is doomed, is the Dark Prince Himself, is a disease that, if not isolated and removed, will certainly infect us all.

Humiliation hollows me out, reveals a sinkhole of self-loathing. But Greggor is unmoved. He abides criticism unflinchingly, as I never can—perhaps why I love him so.

Things that rust: our cast-iron skillet after Mother throws it on the lawn during an epic fight with Da, a bent nail sticking out of the first pew bench at Holy Mary's, a latch on the hard-shell suitcase I packed that time I ran away from home.

Horror and relentless despair!

Greggor has had enough of my *prissy church business* and is going steady with Marie Belanger's bad-girl cousin, Stephanie; the one with the crimped hair. They make out against the school's chain-link fence, and in the alley behind the convenience store, and directly in front of Holy Mary's. Stephanie wears massive shoulder pads like Dynasty's Alexis and leaves outlandish hickies on Greggor's neck, which he showcases in a deep-V Pistons jersey, plus one on his forehead—less sexy, but more defiant: the girl owns him.

I crave his body, the electric current we make. Without it, I wither. I am nothing. Oh sodomy! Yet I fear for my condemned Soul. If I do not confess, if I refuse the Sacrament of Reconciliation, and cannot change my ways where Greggor is concerned, I will burn in the flames of Hell. The Church is my only refuge now, but I'm in no mood for Father Casey's tedious blather. A defiant power, an appetite, grows in me, and Father Casey and the Church are no match.

Like a tongue returning to a sore tooth, Father Casey presses in a fatherly way, impatient and cross—is it school? Trouble at home? God forbid, marijuana? Do I have questions about the liturgy? "Perhaps you've other distractions, at your age." I can hardly say I'm in love with a meathead who dumped me for Stephanie Belanger! He says, "In fact, you're by far the eldest altar boy I've had. Ever heard of, for that matter. Perhaps it's time for a change."

Sacked by the priest. No one will have me, not even the Church! No more mahogany wood or velvet curtains, save what I can see from the civilian pews. Beautiful St Francis of Assis, whom I adore, abandoned inside: the statue I kissed when the nuns weren't looking. After years of devotion, I'm to appear Sunday mornings with the proles. I mope and fantasize escape: the mean city streets might welcome me, *if* I can find them. Toronto, New York, or San Francisco. Anyplace fierce enough to hold the immensity of my boy love. Could there be a fabulous life out there, somewhere, waiting? Outcasts—and I've come to accept this is what I am—have been running away since time immemorial. Why not me?

I pack an on-board flight bag from an airline that no longer exists, the bag Da brought to Canada. Beige with green and orange diagonal stripes, it has worn leather handles and a sticky zipper. The bag holds my new size-eleven dress shoes quite nicely, and hardly anything else. Which means they will not be running away *with* me; not unless I wear them on my already blistered feet, which presents a dilemma—in the war between fashion and comfort, who wants to weigh in on the side of sensible footwear? Not I, certainly. Toothbrush, toothpaste, and mouthwash from the cupboard under the bathroom sink. If I'm running away, I'll need fresh breath. My acne-prone face wash is large but vital. Razor and shaving cream, same. I can't possibly grow a beard, but I hate wisps, so the shaving kit is coming, no question. Two pairs of clean socks, two Y-fronts, my baby-blue Star Wars T-shirt and best Levis, the only ones that fit. I roll the jeans and still can't shut the bag.

Fine. I wear the jeans and Star Wars shirt with a jacket and pack a dress shirt and tie, in case I get a respectable job and don't need to whore myself on the side of the road. The shoes, regrettably, will have to be mailed later, if Mother will agree to pay postage. Or maybe I'll send money once I'm established and properly appreciated and getting handsomely recompensed for my singular perspectives on global politics, art, and culture. For example, after I am hired by the *Globe* to share my extraordinary views with more literate countrymen than populate this sorry town!

I remember the hard-shelled suitcase with its rusty latch, hidden under their bed. It holds a secret stash of whisky, French pantyhose, Chanel lipstick in a questionable shade of red. As far as I know, Da has never thought to look in it. The suitcase is remarkably appropriate—respectable, mature, spacious. A game-changer.

My parents' bedroom is a place of quiet horror. They keep the blind pulled, since the only window faces the

Mastronardis', a couple of feet away. Da painted the window shut two years ago, but refuses to admit it. He pretends he *wants* the window shut all of the time, and so it smells like the pub—cigarette smoke and day-after beer sweats and a hint of that soap. I lift the polka-dotted bed skirts. Underneath is a forgotten, dust-filled crypt the vacuum cleaner never reaches. I sneeze. Drag the suitcase, empty it, notice with surprise there's a different bottle from the last time I snooped, Powers Gold Label, and that it's in fact larger than the previous bottle of Jameson.

The front door slams, opens, slams again.

"Oh, stick your bloody Jesus with a pin." That's Da.

"May He strike you down for saying it," she says.

Mother's heels click on the kitchen linoleum then mute on the living room carpet.

Hefty strides across linoleum, a chair thuds to the floor.

"Don't you touch me," she hisses.

There's a smack. A moan. Uneven tap-clumps down the hall, hurrying this way. She has lost a shoe. Heavy steps follow and I have no choice, I crawl under the bed—the only place large enough to hide me and the suitcase. Flat on my back, my nose grazes the underside of the mattress as they argue and weep and he rips at her blouse, which floats to the carpet in a white puddle. I stare at it while they fuck, right above me. Her crying turns to moans of pleasure, his swearing to wordless grunts. The bed shakes with effort until finally, finally, Da shouts some strangled prayer of release and they collapse into each other, spent.

"Junebug," says Da.

"Yes, lover," she sings.

"Best get the roast in or we'll never eat tonight," he says, and swings his legs over the side of the bed in search of pants.

That's when I sneeze the second time.

Rather than head to confession, I stop at Grandmother's on my way out of town, drop the suitcase, collapse crying and hiccupping, and recount the entire debacle into the filthy anonymity of her coal chute. In olden days, an actual man shovelled coal into the hatch; it's how they heated the place. Later, they switched to electric, but the chute remained; it's part of the house's charm. Hinges squeak and bits of rust flake off when I lift the squat iron door. I prop it open with a stick. A gust of blackened air wafts out: Grandmother's rotted breath from beyond the grave.

Dusk: bats emerge from the chute, flapping hysterically up to the purple sky, and I squeal. A familiar chuckle alerts me, and, sure enough, when I wheel about, there is Himself, wearing the Detroit Red Wings shirt I like best. Gruesome yellow bruises decorate his neckline.

He nods at my suitcase. "Going someplace, God Boy?"

"Running away," I say, wiping my eyes on my sleeve. My goal is to survive the long walk toward the turn-off, where I might hitch a ride to the 401. Toronto is two hundred miles northeast. I've no plan beyond that.

That snaggle-tooth smile and the bulge in his faded jeans unravel me. "Let's go in, first."

Greggor's body brushes mine as he ambles past. I count one-one thousand, two-one thousand, three, and follow him to the veranda, where I set my case. A window-board has been pried off and I clamber over the sill. My sneakers make no noise on Grandmother's debris-scattered floor. All these visits and never once have I trespassed inside. It's so dark. Greggor squeezes my thin arms. Crushes me to his chest. Dull light shines through the one slatted window onto his face, which is an inch from mine. His pupils are engorged, the outer iris dark blue, the inner flecked silver. There's a golden crust of sleep in the corner of one eye, and I want to brush it away.

"Fag God," he whispers.

We kiss.

Ambrosia.

Greggor pushes me onto a rotting antique chair that was once a tremendous, royal-blue velvet. This was the sitting room, a somber and dignified place with an elegant side table where Sybil set out pastries and tea. There had been an old-timey phonograph and a stack of heavy records, pre-vinyl. I'm sure Grandmother bade Sybil to crank the handle while she lay on the matching velvet couch, enraptured by antediluvian operas. I can see her in her pink Chanel pantsuit, nibbling tiny, crustless sandwiches, watching us.

I say, "What about Stephanie?"

"What about her?" He shrugs.

Greggor unzips his jeans. A rodent scampers under the stack of demolished furniture as I take him in my mouth. One salty drop on my tongue. A fly buzzes around my head. I can't swat: my hands hold his sharp hipbones, which thrust with deliberation. One hand grips the back of my head, then the other. I've missed his gentle-rough way of handling me. Little gasps tell me he is nearing climax. Sounds, clear and loud, shoot from his mouth as Greggor bucks and sighs. Sounds that promise he is all mine, that I am his. Beyond that is the call of a crow at some distance, rising and falling, commanding the countryside: caw, caw, caw.

Sanctuary.

After, Greggor says, "You're really leaving?" His face fills with longing. His voice cracks, dust or buried emotion.

I take it to mean he wants me to stay. That this thing with Stephanie Belanger is a simple ruse to stoke my jealousy, that I belong to him like a bride. I'm speechless. If only the Church would quarantine us, so as not to contaminate others with our unnatural perversions. We'd live in these ruins, blissfully undisturbed: a kind of marriage, except happy.

"I'll probably die in this hole," he says.

Pants, open at the waist, fallen around his thighs, Greggor taps a cigarette from his pack and the tiny flare on his face from the lighter is all the gold in the world.

"Oh my God!"

The voice swoops up an octave, sends me scrabbling. Stephanie Belanger's wine cooler smashes on the floor. We straighten clothing, fasten zippers. It's dark, but she's seen enough. Stephanie's hysteria brings other kids running from the yard.

"That's my boyfriend?!"

"Babe, relax," he says to her engorged face. "It's not what you think."

"Die, you sick fucks!"

She throws a chair leg, an empty mickey. I crouch behind the collapsed couch. Two junior football guys appear in the window; they've dumped out my suitcase and hold up each item, howling. "George Michael!" they hoot at my fold-out Wham! poster. "Gayest of lords," they scoff at my shirt and tie. One sprays shaving cream in the other's face. Stephanie hurls something, the metal can, and hits Greggor's temple.

"Shit," he says, as blood trickles. He stands, chest heaving.

Greggor yanks the belt from his hastily zipped jeans and lashes the air, clearing a path to the window. Coward, I creep behind. He hurdles the sill like a gazelle and bolts across the veranda, leaping their case of beer. I trip on the ledge, scramble over the porch railing, land in the spirea. Greggor sprints the laneway; he does not stop, and does not look back. I'll never get away but have one advantage: I know this old house better. I race to the coal chute, still propped open.

In I squeeze, through thick cobwebs, down into the pitch, to the basement. Tiny scramblings on my face and arms have me wildly slapping the hairiest and leggiest of spiders. No doubt I deserve this horror—my perdition! I am pleased to have kept the chute propped open; this small square of light, my only promise. I try to recall the basement layout and steep wooden stairs that lead up to the ground floor, into the kitchen. Once those fanatics leave, I'll make my way back through the house and out the front window, find what's left of my belongings. I crawl, mouth puckered shut, face screwed in terror, through loose, rattling piles of what could only be raccoon shit or decomposing nests, and I would shriek but for fear of discovery—and the phobia of having some unfathomably grotesque insect burrow into my mouth where it'll lay eggs that will later hatch and devour me from the intestines, out.

Sex, boy sex, is obviously to blame!

Is Grandmother looking down, thin nostrils flared in disgust? Or might her spirit protect me, her erstwhile admirer, unlovable and grown into clumsy adolescence? As I inch the cement floor, light emanating from the chute weakens. Eventually, I bump into the staircase and begin to feel my way up, step by creaking step, discovering along the way a long since deceased mouse carcass—at least I presume so by its rigid tail—dried up and stuck to the wood. It is an ascension of sorts, only into more darkness, terror, and confusion. Perhaps I shall scuttle directly into the waiting jaws of the horned Prince Himself, become Satan's bony morsel.

At long last I reach the top. I strain to hear anything, but no.

Maybe they've gone?

My hand finds the doorknob and turns. Nothing. I shake and bash the door. Of course, it's locked, perhaps even nailed shut. Why wouldn't it be? I sit on the top step, sobbing. I will die and dry up and my corpse, too, will adhere to the steps of this ancient staircase. Tragic, and also, how embarrassing!

I sit in the dark, seething.

Much later, it's the honking that wakes me.

Engines thrum and doors slam. A car radio blasts Bon Jovi, which brings me back to my terrible reality. More have come to flush me out: a lynch mob. Thuds—perhaps a two-by-four whacking the boarded-up windows along the side of the house. I pray they won't notice and investigate the coal chute, still propped open, but of course they do. Boys love sticks. They love to poke and stab and hit things. The hinges creak and someone sticks his head into the void.

"We're coming for you, Boy George!"

That warcry rattles my bones, which crumble in terror. He drains a bottle and chucks it down the chute, smashing it on the cement. Scuffling and grunting: he's climbing in. Shouts, "Fawwwwk!" He's stuck halfway. Other boys laugh and hack at the basement window boards, manage to rip one free, shattering a pane of glass. Headlights pour in, illuminating the marks I made like some wounded reptile dragging its sorry carcass across the dirty floor.

The still-stuck boy, one of the Mucci brothers, is hauled out of the chute and razzed mercilessly. "Shut up!" he shouts. "Anyway, he's not down there." He pisses a golden stream through the broken window. *Rock you like a hurricane*, he sings, shaking his penis and tucking it neatly away. Still flustered from misadventure, he doesn't see me only feet away, coal-dusted and draped in webbing at the top of the shadowy stairs like a petrified gargoyle. I want to turn myself in—I am surely on the cusp of a fatal aneurism—but someone shouts, "He's in the orchard!" and the boys get back in their cars, slam the doors, and tear down the laneway.

Alone, again.

Invisible, even to those who despise and hunt me.

I descend the staircase, remove my ruined T-shirt, and wrap my fist in it. Brush away the piss-covered glass shards from the basement window. I saw that in a movie, and it works. I climb past splintering boards. My head and body ache. My throat is raw. Topless, I keep to the shadows and limp the well-treed way home.

Things with obvious beginnings and ends: a ball of yarn unravelled; a Hollywood film; a loaf of bread, sliced and bagged and sealed with a date-stamped tag.

Morning.

Alive, against all odds.

A hot, sudsy shower removes the filth of last night's undoing, but not the countless scrapes and bruises. Today is Holy Mary's annual bake and garage sale, the Friendly Club's euchre tournament. Greggor's words, his electrifying sorrow regarding my departure, gives me strength. But even *he* cannot protect me from a mob of sadistic teens.

The upside: at least we have this calamity uniting us. We'll be the only boys *not* at the tractor pull this afternoon.

Bound together, possibly forever.

In the kitchen, unseemly light streams through curtain frills. Sun on the table, sun spilling onto linoleum, sun fingering its way up the cupboards, up the grease-spackled wall behind the stove. Da paces, his cigarette smoke hazing the room. Mother slams a jar of plum jam on the table, a plate of toast. Eggs are scrambled in the cast-iron pan, which she heaves onto the table. Side-glancing, with crossed arms and fearsome staring—as though I am some odious beast.

"Father Casey's let you go," says Mother.

"Too old," I say, feeling even sorrier for myself. "He's got the Addams' boy now."

"We got a call about Grandmother's place," she says, blanching.

"What about it?" I stammer.

Da barks about military college, cadet school. "It'll make a man of him!"

"People are saying things," Mother says.

"The army. *If* they'll take him," he says.

I can hardly imagine—all those male specimens in uniforms. Greggor could enlist, too.

"Navy," Da concedes. "Could find mercy there."

"Like some others," says Mother.

Her words sever an invisible cord in his gullet.

"What about this other boy," says Da, quietly. "Is that where you got the idea?"

He is somewhat deflated, knuckling the back of his wooden chair, shirt rolled to elbows, revealing gruesome scars and the blue anchor etched on bulbous forearm: permanent souvenirs from his previous life.

He says, "You don't need to broadcast it, son."

Broadcast? I've never told a single person!

"Couldn't he tone it down a little? Who spies on his own parents like that?" Mother starts to cry.

I say, "Tone *what* down? I'm not even fully me!"

"They say Rock Hudson was a gay and look what happened!" Her eyes are huge, framed by wet triangle lashes.

"You're not safe, Pauly," says Mother.

"His name is *Paul*, dammit. You made him this way," Da says.

"I only ever wanted companionship. He's always been excellent company to me."

True enough. I'd been her perfect boy.

Da says, "Say it. Because *I've* never been good enough."

Mouth agape; I'm a hooked fish. Steam wafts from the teapot and the scrambled eggs. The toast is cold. Da drops his fists. Takes his coat from the hook, shuffles into boots. The door shuts behind him.

"You have no idea, either of you," I say. "Hijacking my life."

She sniffs. "Never mind. It'll take some getting used to. Let's eat."

Eat, at a time like this!

I stamp to the living room, where our smug rotary phone nestles beside the couch. Fingers shaking, I dial the number I memorized in grade three. I'm through with this town. I'm all his, completely reborn to sin.

It rings and rings and finally a woman with a dump-truck voice says, "Whaddaya want?"

"Greggor, please."

Labored breathing: she screeches.

I picture her clutching the receiver to oversized bosom. I picture a sleeveless housedress, stained. *Poor Greggor.*

More yelling, a ruckus—his brothers, no doubt.

Then, a grunt by way of salutation. *Him*. Peach fuzz above his scowling lips.

"It's Paul," I say, like a dumbass.

The steady sound of his breath.

"You okay?" I say.

I close my eyes.

"Hardly," he says.

"But you made it home safe." The knot in my belly begins to unwind, just a little.

I say, "Let's leave town. Today."

"What?"

"Come with me. I can't stay."

"I know. Don't call here. I'm not like you," he says.

"Of course you are. We're in this together."

"I said you paid me. To let you, you know," he says.

"I paid you? How much?" I stammer.

"Twenty bucks. Stay away from me," he says. "I fucking mean it."

"Greggor—"

"Anyways, I'm going with Stephanie again."

Pause.

"Sorry," he says.

Dial tone.

"Hello?"

I hang up the phone and sit for a minute or an hour, frozen.

Not in it together, then.

Not bound forever!

Greggor blames *me* for this catastrophe: his complete and utter social ruin. Worse, he blames me for that anomalous kernel of desire chugging its way through his body, down through all his limbs, infecting them.

I press a crocheted pillow to my face. I *would* pay him, but with what? No one will hire me, not with my frailty, my predilection to expand vocabulary rather than to engage with farm animals or team sports.

No more clandestine encounters.

Greggor, my Only: light brown curly hair tickling my skin. Lazy smile on his mean mouth, dirty words flying out it, and thousands of kisses searing my lips. Thick eyebrows and those wonky eyes, striped and flecked, dark and light.

Irrevocable.

Things they will find in my pockets: a mottled dryer sheet; a fossil from Grandmother's woods; a bubblegum wrapper with Greggor's drawing of our two haloed heads with eye dots and smiles—joined by a smeary cross.

Pariah.

Sixteen, utterly friendless, a homicidal wreck. Spiritually unmoored, denied the routine and sanctity of the Church. Despised. Rejected! I had hoped to live long enough to leave a handsome corpse.

Monday at school they will come for me. A warzone. And where to hide in the dread twilight hours? Certainly not downtown, not anywhere near the arcade, home to head-bangers, Neanderthal druggies. Not the Legion, where moustachioed seniors buy glasses of rye for a pittance.

All I have: what else?

The conspirator-nuns. The whole town. I'm pitted against all I was raised to embrace and a darkness devours my heart.

There is no other way.

"Gird me, O Lord, with the cincture of purity and extinguish in my heart the fire of concupiscence." I work on the letter, an eternity. Tear down my bedroom poster collage: goodbye Madonna and New Order, goodbye Ian Curtis. Search for rope—we've no pills, and I hate blood. Spy the plant holder from Mother's hanging fern. The macramé is rougher and spindlier than Father Casey's cincture. Half hitch-knotted, unknotted, figure of eight.

Will it hold all one hundred and eighteen pounds?

I stand on the lard bucket to wrestle the massive, glowering plant to the unmopped floor. Step back up. Untwine the whipping, loosen the diagonal lash. Bowline. Slip knot. Noose under my chin. Before me, the full-length mirror. Behind me, the pantry: our broom against the ironing board, that creaking disaster hauled out before Mass and on the eve of special events: weddings, court appearances, funerals.

Footsteps.

Someone coming up the walk.

My knee buckles, shoe slips. My full weight falls on the rope, too soon. My goodbye letter is meant to be in my pocket, not on the shelf. Neck burns, throat closes. Hands fly up. Legs jerk, body swings, frantic. Canned goods knock into each other, hit the ground, rolling. Other sounds: shouting, wrenching the door.

Da calling.

"Paul!"

A jar smashes. My chest heaves, straining. Pressure builds in my eye sockets. I spin. A wilderness opens inside of me, unleashes a rage I didn't know existed, a fire not completely extinguished by an avalanche of childhood terror and adolescent regret. I can still taste his freckled shoulders, the salt trail on his flat stomach, his chin stubble.

Then: strong arms around me. My body cradled as Da cuts me down, loosens the knot. "What have ye done?" He rocks me back and forth in those gnarled, tattooed arms, beard scruff against my cheek. Me, gasping, coughing, held by my father for the first time in ten years.

He can stand to touch me?

"Shh, shh," he says of my noisy lament. "We're alright, lad," he says, and crushes me close. Mother running from her bedroom. Tears and snot, the three of us hold tight. The yellow pantry swirls like daylight, like lemon loaf, like fireworks shooting behind my eyelids when I rub them hard, trying to wake up.

Midnight Meat

MIDNIGHT.

Devil music from the Hellmouth next door.

Lowlife rowdies!

Jonesy swallows two sleeping pills, not one, and stuffs her ears with toilet paper. Clamps on the furry blue earmuffs she wears ice-skating. They block out the brunt, but amplify every stuttered tick inside her head: sniffling, swallowing, grinding. She flops onto her mattress, onto the quilt Mother made. She breathes in, holding it for as long as possible, scrunching her fingers and toes, all her muscles, even her face. When the air finally bursts out, her whole body relaxes. Stevie taught her, and it helps. Pills do, too. Despite drum thunder, an electric guitar assault, and evil laughter from the apartment on the other side of the bedroom wall, her mind darkens. Drifts.

Later, much later, in the black syrup of sleep—a crash.

Jonesy clutches the lace-frill neck of her nightie. Beyond the bedroom are sounds of struggle, floundering, like an animal going down slow. Cabinet doors creak open, slam shut. Slurping and snuffling and the smacking of predator lips.

5:01 a.m. Armed with a cell phone, whose blue halo lights the way, Jonesy jams on slippers, grabs her emergency sling bag, and tiptoes into the darkened main room.

Someone is in her kitchen humming *The Love Boat* theme song.

A flick, and the intruder is washed in fluorescent glow. A tall, longhaired man turns blinking, mouth full, hand rammed knuckle-deep in her Oreo cookie bag, tearing it. Canned soup and Kraft Dinner and the new low-sodium crackers are dumped on the counter. Her Christmas Drambuie, the only liquor on the premises, cap off, lies on its side, dripping. This guy. Completely unashamed to be wearing shorts with his pale, putrid stick legs, gorging himself on her personal property.

Jonesy says, "Hungry?"

Eyebrows thick like caterpillars waggle up and down, nodding. They are lustrous. Does he comb them?

"How'd you get in?"

"Huh?" he says.

She repeats herself, although with her tongue thick with sedative, sloppy without her dentures, it doesn't sound right.

"Oh. Party," he says, thumbing the front door.

It's ajar and the chain lock hangs flaccid.

Did she forget? She is vigilant about securing the perimeter before bedtime.

Outside: voices, raucous laughter, and a particularly high-pitched shriek, probably female. The party is still going strong. How could she have slept through it, music and all? Ganja billows in the hallway, poisoning everyone on the fourteenth floor.

"Uh-oh," she says. "You better go."

Skinny Legs stacks three Oreos in his mouth at once. "Or what?" Crumbs spray onto his Metallica T-shirt and then onto the beige kitchen tiles.

"Or else."

Tingly fingertips, swirling dark spots behind eyelids; she's coal-hot but white in the face.

Skinny Legs tosses the cookie bag onto the counter. It looks like a grenade has gone off, bursting the organized layers of corrugated paper and see-through plastic tray. He saunters close. Very close. Still chewing, he points at her Tweety Bird slippers and says, "I tawt I taw a puddy tat!"

"Jesus, Mary, and Joseph," she says.

Skinny Legs pumps his elbows into the air and clicks his heels. He does the Woody Woodpecker laugh and dashes out the door. Jonesy slams and double-locks, face presses the peephole. Out in the hallway, Skinny Legs smiles and waves. "Th-th-th-that's all folks!"

He's gone.

Empty hallway.

Jonesy exhales.

Then Skinny Legs pops back in view, making her shriek, eyeball against his side of the peephole, bloodshot and darting. He says, "I'll be ba-ack!"

"Over my dead body," she shouts, and she wish wish wishes she hadn't said that. She crosses herself with the power of the Father and Son and Holy Spirit.

Protect me now, Jesus, she thinks.

But it's Mary who comes, as usual. Slithering the tiled wall of the kitchen, her stained blue veil slipping on matted hair. She chews a cigarette between yellowed teeth, lights it off the gas stove, before exhaling, exhaling, filling the room with her smoke. Her lip curls, she shrugs the mantle off her bare shoulders. Says, "How you doin', Jonesy, did you miss me?"

"No. No. I did not. Not exactly."

Jonesy focuses on the worn brown threads of the couch upholstery. Rocks back and forth. Her hands tremble. Sling bag: Ontario health card, birth certificate, ODSP worker's card, Stevie's business card, fold-up grabber, all her pills and, finally, her puffer. Jonesy inhales, her chest as ravaged as the cookie bag.

"Five-elephant, four-elephant, three-elephant, two-elephant, one-elephant."

Puff.

Mary hitches her blue gown. "Think you can ignore me?"

"Yes?"

Mary's stained bare feet rise up, her body is lighter than air. "I've been worshipped and scorned for two thousand years. *Nobody* ignores me." She smokes, is smoke.

Stevie says not to puff more than once, but sometimes Jonesy has to, just to settle her nerves. She does it again and again, until the heaviness shifts in her lungs. Mary floats by the pressboard ceiling. Her phone. Jonesy calls Stevie's office and hangs up. Calls and hangs up. Calls and leaves a convoluted message, but of course Stevie's not there, it's the crack of dawn. Why won't she give Jonesy her cell phone number? She calls Security but Cody is on break and what do you expect. She dials 911 and the dispatcher grills her, as though *she* were the culprit, not the victim in this particular situation: a break and enter in the middle of the night, a grocery theft, a strange man. No mention of Mary, who whispers in her ear the whole time: "I come with maternal intercession to heal the infirm, comfort the afflicted, offer a refuge for sinners." She's muddling things, that Mary, causing Jonesy to shout. Finally, the dispatcher says a patrol car will be coming to check for anything suspicious.

"Ma'am," says Jonesy, "there are plenty of suspicious things happening in this building owned and operated by the Medallion Corporation, and although they are technically liable for unit 1429, I remain alone with God."

"God!" sneers Mary.

Jonesy hangs up.

Churning, churning in her belly and her anus begins to pucker. She gallops to the bathroom and barely makes it in time: a spew of burning liquid explodes into the bowl. "Uh-oh," she says, and grits her teeth for the next deluge, rocking back and forth on the commode. There's cheering next door—for the sounds coming out of her backside or because a song they love has come on, she's not sure.

They sing, *Run to the hills!*

And, *Sink the pink!*

The number of the beast!

Heathens.

Fever lights up her ears, her forehead: probably a virus. Skinny Legs touched her cupboards, doorknobs, groceries, and the refrigerator. He touched her shoulder while she was wearing her nightie, and he definitely pointed at her slippers, which means all of it will have to be put into the basement incinerator due to contamination.

How now, with Disability as her only income and the Trust run out?

She flushes once, twice, and sets about purifying the washroom with Lysol wipes. Stevie says not to use them on personal areas *of the flesh*, but what does she know about male intruders? Just hearing them next door makes Jonesy feel dirty. Mary won't do anything, just snickers until she's so bored she dissipates in one foul yawn. The police never come. Nobody helps. It takes more pills and a very long time to fall back asleep.

Quite late on Sunday, disgruntled and drug-fogged, Jonesy finds Cody snoozing on a chair in front of the ground-floor fire exit, which is propped open with a can of old paint.

"Wake up," she says, "there's been an invasion."

"The Americans?"

Jonesy says, "No, a greasy long-hair. A headbanger."

The school bus had been full of them; the group home, too. That was so long ago, but they look just the same—tight jeans, puffy sneakers, jean jacket, and the bushy hair, shorter at the front and sides, longer at the back. Smoking and swearing and drinking and tormenting.

Bad boys.

Her description: "In his 30s or 20s, hard to tell. Terrifying legs, like dimpled chicken. White and pink and blue, no feathers. A little facial hair."

Cody says, "A goatee?"

"Well I'm not sure," she says.

Cody says there are many types of facial hair. He pulls out a wee notebook from his blue shirt pocket. Doodles with his crossword pen. An oval with a full beard. "No," she says. An oval with a handlebar moustache. "No," she says. Hair all the way around an open mouth, like an obscene drawing. "No no no," she says. She takes her own pen from the sling bag and draws what she remembers.

"Yep, that's a goatee," says Cody. He clips his pen in the folded newspaper where he's been doing the puzzle. Flips the notebook shut and slips it back into his breast pocket.

Cody's uniform is always clean and pressed, at least when he starts his shift. His wife does the laundry but she hates ironing, hates the detailed heat of it. He admitted once that he secretly likes it when the steam hisses out like a dangerous machine, or a dragon.

"Crossword," says Jonesy.

"Yep, I'm stuck."

No surprise.

"Well?" she says. "What about my break and enter?

Cody says, "Could be the guy I found sleeping on a dryer in the laundry room today."

Cats and homeless persons have been known to do the same thing in this building. "Did you notify the authorities?"

"Naw. Seemed harmless," says Cody, and he hoists his boots back on top of the paint can. "He left when I asked him to."

"I feel the need for police protection," she says.

"Oh, Jonesy, you probably don't. They're not all they're cracked up to be. Besides, they're busy with families and obligations as well as fighting crime."

"Criminals. In the city of Toronto. Don't I know, half of them live here at the Medallion Corporation."

Cody laughs, but she's not joking.

"Gotta go," she says, because, wouldn't you know it: churning, churning gut twists. It'll be hard to make it back to the fourteenth floor in time.

At bedtime, Jonesy attends seriously to her duties: windows shut and locked, front door double-locked, perishables stacked neatly in the refrigerator. Check, check, check. Counters wiped clean, sinks plugged to keep out cockroaches. Dentures soaking. Phone charged. Pills swallowed. Sling bag on the bedside table.

It's quiet next door.

The rowdies are too hungover to sing along with their records or even to watch a movie with gunfire and explosions and lots of screaming. Not good for her nerves.

Lights off, shadows creep the bedroom. This is the loneliest time. When she was a little girl, Mother used to knit and sing in her rocker, and Father would read the news, the crinkling and flapping of those large pages lulled her gently to dream. That was a long time ago, before they got old and infirm and sent their only child, Jonesy, who was an overgrown handful, to the group home for safekeeping.

A *headcase*, what the kids at school said.

Jonesy pictures her parents driving the old Ford along Highway 2, on their way to visit. Purse on Mother's lap, gloved fingers holding the strap; Father's hands on the wheel. Tonight she cannot summon them, no matter what. She has scoured the bathroom and kitchen and sterilized the doorknobs, but Skinny Legs left an indelible stain. *Harmless*. Easy for Cody to say. Skinny Legs may as well be sitting on the edge of Jonesy's mattress, staring, touching her all over. Would he? Who can say.

"Sure he would, the sly dog," says Mary from the closet, her voice muffled by the thick fabrics of Jonesy's winter gear. "Horndog."

"Not you again," says Jonesy.

The sliding door jiggles in its track, squeaking as it opens.

"Think I'd leave with a man on the premises?" With dark, furrowed eyes, Mary sucks on her knobby finger and waggles it suggestively.

"Bedtime," says Jonesy. "Besides, he's gone."

"I still smell him," Mary says, shaking out her hair, her skeletal shoulders, her pointy witch teats. "A rare treat. Mary merry meat."

She clops into the room naked: two hooves—that's new—the swish of a long tail, the deep animal scent of her furred haunches. Pale hands twitch in the blue-black. Mary's pooch of a belly, sharp pelvic bones, her thick pair of horse thighs curl and settle next to Jonesy on the squeaky bed. Ancient, sagging breasts, soft as snakeskin, press against her. Stench of decay from that rotting mouth.

"I'm guarding you tonight," she grumbles. Tail flick in the eye; Jonesy tears up.

"Uh-oh." Sharing the bed with Mary, it's the worst. Blanket hog. Drooler. Snoring and humping and who knows what else!

This calls for pills plus her puffer plus the breathing exercise. Fingers of light shine through the split curtain from the hundreds of tiny windows in the new condo facing her building. When the condo people flick them on, one by one, it reminds Jonesy of stars twinkling in the country sky over the farm, back where she grew up.

"God Bless all of my loved ones," she says to the mostly dark room, to the air, to the ghosts of the infinite universe.

Mary farts a loud blast of disapproval. "There's your God, take a whiff."

"Abide with me while I pray for sleep in this long night of trials, to relieve me of my earthly concerns, and protect me from illness and injury and misfortune and disease. God, please please, also protect me from Skinny Legs."

"Church and state like girls to mate. Nighty-night. Don't let the bed bugs bite," says Mary, and hooks her arm around the flubbery folds of Jonesy's belly, practically paralyzing her.

The elevator breaks.

Jonesy is trapped in unit 1429 at the Medallion Corporation without police protection. Monday, Tuesday, Wednesday, Thursday: the days tick. Nights are the worst. No Stevie: she comes next week. She doesn't even return Jonesy's calls, and now her voicemail is full with news of Skinny Legs. No visitors, not unless you count Cody, who knocks to special-deliver a new crossword, and Mary, who appears late and bedraggled, trying to get a look at him.

"Skinny Legs said 'I'll be back,' and I believe him," says Jonesy.

Cody says, "Have you actually *seen* him?"

She frowns. "Neither hide nor hair."

"I'd like to take a look at *his* hide," snickers Mary, her blackened tongue licking the length of the linoleum beside

Cody's boot. "You know what they say about men with big feet."

Jonesy blanches. Two pink circles burn in the centre of her cheeks.

Not again.

"Everything okay?" says Cody.

"True crimes," Jonesy says, but the idea is lost. Something about statistics, things Cody should know. Jonesy can't think with Mary dancing barefoot in the kitchen, singing *Love to Love You, Baby.*

"What can I say? There's only me and Azul to check twenty-nine floors," says Cody.

"Uh-oh." She's woozy, and the tremors start up.

"Can I call someone for you?"

"No," she whispers. Her hands are shaking so much it's hard to double-lock the door behind him. Stevie says these are side effects of the drugs they gave her at the home. Tranquilizers. Anti-psychotics. Who knows what-all. Firecrackers whizz and pop behind her eyes. Head shrinks, crackles; the pain is electric. Arms and legs drum against the kitchen floor, skull rattles loose.

After the seizure, collapsed on the shoe mat in a puddle of urine, it comes to her. "True crimes. Many heinous acts of violence occur in the hours before dawn." To top it off, this is when Cody is largely unavailable.

"You see," she blurts.

"Obviously," Mary shrugs. She's staring down from the ceiling.

"You stayed," says Jonesy.

Mary points. "There's puke in your hair."

For peace of mind, Jonesy sets her alarm for 3 a.m. to reinforce the perimeter, despite a bad knee and her continued suffering from Skinny Legs' virus. Inspection of the premises reveals no burglaries, attempted or otherwise, but plenty of pollution next door. *Ganja! Burnt toast! Late-night popcorn!* She writes it all down in a spiral notebook. Sits vigil on the couch. Reminds her of the day she waited on the group-home porch for her frail parents while the sun inched east to west across the sky. They were never late. Lunch, supper, she wouldn't budge. Had to be dragged in at curfew. She fought them all. There were restraints, injections, a stint back in the psych ward; she was inconsolable. It was weeks before anyone told her about the accident, long past the joint funeral. Back to her lists. Grunt-work frustrates Mary: cleaning, counting, checking the time. The organized mind is no place for her fecund, primordial, despicable Self.

Jonesy wonders: will she be murdered and hacked to bits in her own ceramic tub by first-class maniacs? She's seen it on TV.

"Yes!" Mary promises.

"Shh," says Jonesy, settling back into bed.

Why did she ever come to this terrible city? Lately, Jonesy has been thinking back to her birthplace.

"That shithole," says Mary. "Really."

Wide open sky, horizon punctuated by windmills and grain elevators and telephone poles laced with black wire. Clumps of trees lining the deep roadside ditches. Green in the summer, gold in the fall. Grey and white all winter. Anything else, she can't recall.

"I'll tell you what else." Mary crows loud and shrill, just like Benedict Arnold, their old Copper Maran. Head bobbing, she rooster struts back and forth in the bedroom.

Sometimes the farm appears in extraordinary detail when Jonesy stares at shadows on her wall. If you want something bad enough, you find a way. She cranks her window open and smells the manure spread on thawing fields.

Diesel, gasoline. Squawking from the henhouse. Seed corn slipping between fingers, the metal pail banging against her thigh. This is the best way to fall asleep, pills or no pills: belonging to another time and place entirely.

Jonesy strokes the quivering nostrils of their knobby-kneed horse, Jacob. The hot snort of his breath on her ticklish palm. She digs for the carrot in one pocket, then the other. Did she leave it on the porch? Drat.

Loud sounds: not hooves stamping the stall, it's thumping on the bedroom wall.

Not Father calling to feed the hens, it's another man shouting, "Sonofabitch!"

"Dumbass!" and "Cock-Knobbler-Cunt-Sac!" and other atrocities are being screamed through the wall, the air, the earmuffs, the toilet paper, her skull, into her brain. Men shoving men? Punching? What if they break the drywall and end up in her purple bedroom with the pony carousel lamp? Annihilation.

Now she's awake and worried, and who wants to lie in bed while yardbirds go at it next door? Bedside clock says 4:23 a.m. Jonesy takes precautions. She brings her sling bag and phone into the living room.

"Help!" A man's voice in the hall.

Skinny Legs?

Jonesy uses her puffer and takes an anxiety pill. She presses against the peephole. A body lying on the Medallion Corporation's unclean carpet. Sneakers and red track pants with white stripes. She unlocks the door but leaves the chain on, the way Stevie showed her. Voilà, the man's rounded belly rising and falling in his matching red jacket. Still can't see his face. Jonesy unchains, steps out, breathless.

"Skinny Legs?" she says.

No. Too bad. An older man with greying dreadlocks and

a steak knife stabbed through his hand and blood blood blood.

She says, "Are you a ghost?"

"Not yet. Got a smoke?"

"I don't smoke. I have asthma and I am trying to breathe properly and your blood knife is not helping!"

The knife is stuck through his palm into the carpet and floor.

He says, "Give me a hand?"

"How about a glass of water?"

He says, "Okay but if you find some whisky, I'll take that instead."

She closes and chains the door, twists the lock. Should she call Stevie? The police? What's the point, they never come. Finds a plastic cup she hates, guests only, fills it with tap water. Counts out loud to forty-four (chlorine). When she opens the door to the hallway again, no Grey Ghost. Did she invent him? But the torn carpet hosts a dark stain. Should she leave the water? She decides to forget it; that guy is long gone now.

Inside again, she dumps the water, drips in bleach and soap for obvious germ reasons. Sets the cup in the sink for sterilization. Dials Security, but surprise, Cody does not answer. Probably asleep. Before he came to Medallion he used to slice meat at the all-night butcher's on Bloor Street. You'd think he'd be used to staying up.

"Meat, meet the butcher's knife." Mary materializes, face-down, on the living room carpet. Her mantle spills and gathers around her armpits. She humps her bony ass in the air, shudders and moans, works the slick path between her thighs. "Meat, meet the butcher's wife!"

"Uh-oh." Times like these Jonesy thinks about living in this world without parents, God Bless them in Heaven, and it's hard.

"How hard is it?" pants Mary, the letch.

After they sold the farm and before the accident, they put money in trust to pay for the private group home in Brampton. Eleven years, then it ran out. Her own bedroom but no lock, no keys. The man-handed night nurse weekdays, and the bald one, the shifty-eyed ratface, every weekend, a real meany. After her parents died, things got worse—impunity without visitors. Jonesy writes in the notebook, pressing so hard her pen nib tears the page. Eleven, 11, 1 + 1. 11111111111111. 1 infinity, forever.

"Boner-kill," says Mary. She collapses, flat-backed. Tufts of pubic hair, green streaked with grey, coil with resentment. "Where was your God then?" Her eyes fix on Jonesy.

"Numbers, numbers," says Jonesy.

"Can't trust a man, not even Himself."

"Mother of penitent sinners," says Jonesy.

"What I try and do for you."

"Leave me be."

"Never!" Mary stomps onto the couch beside Jonesy and steps right through the picture window behind her, fourteen floors up, vanishing into the early creep of dawn.

"Whew."

The clock ticks, kitchen faucet drips.

It's quiet without Mary.

Maybe Jonesy will go outside. She's afraid to leave her unit but afraid to stay in, too. Every other Tuesday, when she comes for the forcible injection for the so-called schizophrenia, Stevie says she should *venture out more*. What does Stevie know? The city of Toronto is not Jonesy's birthplace! She's trapped here with her disease.

They fix the elevator: Hallelujah! Jonesy needs groceries, plus Immodium for loose stools. There's a new pharmacy and grocery store across the street for all the condo magazine people. In the creaking elevator, Jonesy tries to not breathe (germs), but people squeeze in on each floor: Marguerite with her walker, Thomas and his two yappy dogs, Celia and her senile mother, who pushes all the buttons, making the alarm ring. Jonesy is running out of air. On the eighth floor, lo and behold, Skinny Legs. Wearing long pants, he's a real hubba hubba.

Our Lord and Saviour!

Skinny Legs grins. "Got any more cookies?"

Her cheeks are bursting. She'll definitely have to open her mouth before they reach the lobby.

He says, "What are you doing?"

She shakes her head.

"Seriously. What the hell, lady."

"Ah!" Jonesy gasps contaminated air. She holds it in the rest of the way. Skinny Legs points at her Sylvester cat lapel pin and Jonesy says, "Touch it and I will scream."

He jumps out when the doors open on the ground floor. "Where ya headed?"

"Groceries. I've been trapped in my unit like a captive. A bad knee and other personal problems, thanks to your break and enter."

"Huh. I'm going there too," he says.

Jonesy makes the sign of the cross. *Mother of the forsaken, protector of all whom the world despises, please do not rebuke me*. Jonesy unzips her bag to get the Dollar Store grabber, and pokes his arm. He *is* real!

"Just checking," she says. "Do I know you from the city of Toronto or from the farm?"

He says, "The funny farm. What about those Oreos?"

"They had to be destroyed, along with everything else you touched with your dirty fingers in my personal private apartment."

He says, "No way."

"Way."

He says, "Not like you need more cookies anyway."

"What's that supposed to mean?"

But she knows exactly what he's getting at and it is none of Skinny Legs' beeswax. For the record, her Dad used to say she was big-boned, like a farm girl ought to be. Jonesy has always been sturdy, at least until recently. Now she's wobbly, insubstantial. Not reliable.

Skinny Legs flips his stringy brown hair and begins to whistle.

"Hellshock." Jonesy sounds out the evil-fonted letters on his shirt.

"It's a band," he says.

"It's what you give me: electrocuting zaps from Hell."

"Sweet," he says, "ha ha."

But she's not even joking.

Sometimes Stevie asks if men ever *bother* her. "Of course," Jonesy says, "man turds bother everyone." Stevie blushes and asks about girl and boy-parts, and *good touching* versus *bad touching*, and something about *consent*. Jonesy is a grown adult, a middle-aged woman who can do as she likes. But Stevie still asks, does she engage in *intercourse*? Does she use *protection*? Girl talk! Jonesy giggles, hides her face. Kicks her feet a bit. Stevie and Mary have something in common, they're always going on about her downstairs mix-up.

At the store, Jonesy snaps on latex gloves before touching the shopping basket. She travels all the aisles except the meat and deli areas, which are rife with bacterial infections, not to mention dead animals. How Cody could've been a part-time butcher is beyond her. He is, otherwise, a very nice man. Smoke rises from the meat counter: Holy Mary, Mother of God, Queen of Heaven and Earth.

Jonesy will have to hurry if she wants to shop without interference.

Jonesy's cell phone dings, and a smiley-face notification appears: *eat more veggies!* Stevie programmed reminders; she's always talking about vegetables for the sugar diabetes, but what does she know? Wrapped in plastic, dried out. Or else dumped on a counter, covered in germs. Nothing tastes fresh from the farm. Sometimes Jonesy buys a tomato and its pink, thick flesh makes her weep.

Cream of mushroom soup is on sale but the only cans left are too far back on the shelf.

"Meep meep." Skinny Legs trots up behind her, pushing a cart. Inside are two six-packs of Budweiser and a bag of Funyons.

"Vitamins," says Jonesy.

"Exactly," he says.

A waft of burnt toast. The darkening cloud looms. One dirty bare foot then the other materializes to caress the canned vegetables lining the top shelf. Our Lady of Sorrows! Jonesy fans herself with the in-store flyer.

"Fish sticks are on sale," Skinny Legs says, oblivious to the hairy calves and bruised thighs descending beyond his head.

"Barbarian." Jonesy reaches for a soup can on tippy toes.

"Allow me," says Skinny Legs.

"Germs!"

"Hmm." Skinny Legs frowns while he thinks. "Aha." He uses a box of crackers to bat a few soup cans close to the edge. The sparse hairs at the corner of his mouth are stained orange, maybe spaghetti sauce.

Mary knots her robe waist high, points a black-tipped finger at Jonesy, and cackles with delight. "Lick it up, buttercup!"

Jonesy carefully peels off one glove. She wets her thumbprint and rubs the spot on his face until it comes clean. His lips twitch. A sort of smile. She'd say something, but what? All the words she knows are trapped between her dry-bitten lips, her unpredictable throat, her wildly thumping bosom. Or way, way down, in the swirling, unnerved world tucked beneath her belly for safekeeping.

Asset Mapping in Stoop City

(for Wendy Babcock)

STOOP, stoop, stoop, stoop.

Everyone's parked on their shitty front steps, smoking, sipping coffee, stretching and yawning and praying for a breeze. Everyone's got a radio with their own crap music: gangsta rap and classic rock. One loser blasts new country. Sheila stomps past them all, the long block north.

"Hey! You seen my feather earrings?"

A shrivelled-up guy with tattoos scrawled on forehead and neck and skinny, wrinkly arms raises his Coffee Time cup like a cheers.

"Who the fuck are you?" she says.

She stooped *somewhere* last night, made some coin, some new friends. Things are fuzzy. She remembers Gord appearing, kicking up a fuss and dragging her home at dawn. Fighting about some bearded guy, loud-mouthed and big-bellied. Not bad-looking, she remembers thinking.

Maybe the party had been the next street over.

"Fuckers!"

Sheila turns and stomps all the way back, beelines for the corner of Lansdowne and Dupont. Her corner. She rocks heel-toe, heel-toe, making her hair swing, she's so mad. Good earrings gone, purse empty. Stabworthy hangover. Plus she's already been kicked out of the Coffee Time this morning. Who cares, she's sick of that place, that guy wants to call the cops, let him. Loser. And who cares, now she's officially *off the fucking property line*, okay, she's on the public property sidewalk.

"Okay?!"

Morning traffic and it's not too hot out yet so somebody is going to want a little love, no doubt about it. She swings her sharp hips. Arms flail and she tries to rein them in, cross them in front or let one hand hold the other, fingers twitching. Her arms do what they want these days. Bubblegum helps with the jaw, can't stop chewing. One decent thing Gord did was give her the rest of his pack of Juicy Fruit. Up in the overheated room on the seventeenth floor, Gord is holding out on her. And they better not smoke the whole stash while she's down here. They better not or she will fucking destroy them. Fucking Gord.

Twenty bucks would do it, even ten.

Five's a foil hit, but she needs more.

A silver SUV slows and Sheila twirls so he can get a good look. Tinted windows rolled all the way up equals air conditioning, good news. She wants a twenty, hand job is okay, she'll use her mouth a bit to get him hard, the usual. She hates swallowing, it burns her throat and gurgles her stomach and gives her the shits and then she's out of commission for the rest of the day, no thank you mister. Sheila does a few high kicks so the driver can see how nice her legs are, guys always tell her, plus she's wearing her lucky white jean shorts that used to be so tight her ass cheeks peeked out, but she's skinny now, not much in the caboose.

"Hey guy," she waves.

High kick.

The man in the car stares but does not wave back.

"What are ya, shy?" she hollers.

The stoplight changes to green. The car speeds away from her and Sheila screeches, "Fuck you, man!"

There goes her money. That guy just left with her money, he robbed her.

She swings around the bus stop pole and who cares about that fag, she's looking great and there will be another guy in another car, someone better. Pest-control truck: Sheila turns her back and pretends to study the bus schedule. She's not doing him, forget it. Probably bugs all through the seats, probably bugs all over that guy. She had them at her old place and that was a frigging disaster. Had to dump all her shit. Lost everything, more or less, that's what you get with bugs. That's how she ended up with Gord at Crack Towers.

All she has left is a plastic bag with her favourite jeans and that pink sparkly princess top and the plastic jelly sandals with the wedge heel. Not throwing those out, forget it. Everything else abandoned, gone to the dump, burned, whatever they do with garbage. Her whole waiting-room magazine collection and everything.

Sheila sits on the bench inside the bus shelter, hand covering her face. It's stuffy inside but so what. The truck is still there, farting diesel out its flappy muffler at the red light. "Forget it, guy!" she yells through her fingers. The sun is creeping higher, blazing between high rises, burning a path all the way across the parking lot into the bus shelter, heating yellow strips of her flesh. She licks her lips: thirsty.

When she got turfed from that mental boarding home the social worker said she didn't pay the rent. Liar. Said her *lifestyle choices endangered* the other women. Said she should know better *at her age*, that she wasn't a teenager anymore, this was *real life*. Sheila made a lot of money up there; of course she paid rent. And those psycho chicks are not endangered, they're a dime a dozen, so what. Probably went through her stuff, bugs and all, probably fought over her room after Sheila took off. It was pretty nice, a window and everything. Private up on the top floor of the ramshackle old house. Hot though, no air conditioning, so sometimes all she could do was crank open the window and crawl out to the coal-hot fire escape to catch a night breeze. Lick the salt from her sweaty upper lip, mop her hairline. It was hard to open that window, and once it was open you couldn't really shut it, but you could see the tip of the church spire from there, and at night with all the lights on it looked like Disneyland, a place she's never been but she's seen the commercials and hey, maybe, you never know. She's pretty bummed now, thinking about all the stuff she left behind. A bedazzled mirror from the Dollar Store with fuzzy pink trim spelling out *Gorgeous!* The last of her old sketchbooks: art school, a lifetime ago, when she first came to this city, gonzo. All the shitty things those chicks could be doing. Laughing at her drawings or selling her clothes or cutting up her magazines. Those bitches.

She should march right down there and see for herself. Straight down Lansdowne into the middle of Parkdale, pretty far, but she did it on cheque day, looking for her money. Helluva mix-up due to not telling her worker about moving—Sheila dreaded dealing with the *new* worker assigned to the *new* neighbourhood, who would demand to see figments of her long-lost ID. ID with her *old* name, the one she never goes by anymore, never tells to a soul.

Sheila gets so riled up thinking about how some other chick is in that room, the nicest room she'd had in a long time, with the view. The view was real good and the fire escape came right up under the window. She could go in and out, never mind a key, just do her own thing and invite the guys up that way. Saved going down the stairs to buzz them in. She made good money up there; barely had to leave the joint. Should have hid her money better. That was a sad day. Gord said she was a dumb cunt and *I told you so* and disappeared for two weeks on an epic bender, he was so mad.

A fucking racket coming down the sidewalk—an old broad wearing a garbage bag pushing a shopping cart piled with empties. Sheila jumps up and covers her ears with her twitchy hands. She paces back and forth on the sidewalk.

"Shaddup, shaddup! Shaddup, can queen!"

She can't even think.

"Ahhhh!"

Sheila marches through the parking lot. She should go inside; not fair she has to listen to this; she's trying to work. She presses her face against the donut shop's glass door, breathes a round oval on the smudged glass. That same turd is still behind the counter. He picks up the phone and waves it, eyebrows two angry slashes. She's not in the mood for cops today, that is some total bullshit. She barely hit him anyway. It was more of a tap. No marks or nothing, but who will the cops believe? Not her!

She marches back across the parking lot, arms swinging, and that can queen is crossing the street heading for the beer store. Thing is, once you start collecting cans, no one will fuck you. Some people say Sheila has a crappy job, but canning is way worse: that's for when your pussy dries out. No teeth is still good for gummies, no excuse. Sheila knows an old broad who still rakes it in on cheque day, working the stairwell at the motel. Good for her. Although it cuts into the competition. Gord says she ought to charge *more* on cheque day not *less*, coz that's when guys got their money. "Everyone loves to spend," Gord says. "Look at 'em, lined up at the corner store for soda and pork rinds and smokes. They should be dropping it on us. It's our money."

Sheila says, "I don't know."

Better to have a ten than a five.

Better to have five than nothing.

Another red light and there's a new line of shiny cars, sun bouncing off them like rhinestones. Lots of cars means lots of men. Sheila lifts her T-shirt and presses against the heated passenger window of one of them. Her tits aren't big but lots of guys go for it. Some prefer a flat chest, they tell her that all the time. "Hey you want some tit, you want some good tit times," she yells. "Come on, guy," and then she says, "what the fuck are you, a guy or what?" The chick driver honks at her. Fucking chicks. Sheila shouts, "You look like a dude, what can I say," and now other cars are also honking, it's confusing. She's between the car lanes and everyone's so mad, so fucking mad in the morning. Jesus. If anyone should be mad it's Sheila, ripped off again by that dickshit Gord and his junkie loser friends.

Someone yells, "Get off the road, lady!"

"I'm trying to make some money," she yells back.

"Off the road!"

"A blow job is better than no job!"

Sheila heard that from a chick who used to give out free condoms—a nice idea, but most dudes say *forget it*, they shrinkydink right up. So really you're just losing money on a supposed freebie. Sheila high kicks a few times. She's got great legs, they should know. Someone might pull into the parking lot. Might want a quickie before work or on their morning break. It happens. Not at lunch though; the concrete bakes so hot your sneakers melt. Streets empty out, even the pigeons vanish. The parking lot dumpsters radiate their stink and no one's thinking about sex in that heat.

But night-time or the morning after, maybe. They could be sitting at their work, whatever it is, what the hell would any of these people do for money? Them sitting and thinking about her legs and her flat titties and they could decide they want to spend a little time with Sheila. The important thing is not to give up.

"Make the most of your assets," the social worker at the old house told her once, and Sheila agrees. If you've got a great ass, show your ass. Let 'em know what you've got straight up and don't waste anyone's time. She's all business that way. She's no liar. Sheila's got a set of pins on her but not so much in the tits and ass department, not like back in the day, when she had a booty. When she first got to Toronto guys were freaked out by her bleached hair, her heavy eyeliner, the creepy things she said. But once she toned down the Goth weirdo arty shit, did she ever rake it in. Gord didn't have the nerve to even *talk* to her back then, she was so far outta his league.

Guys couldn't get enough of her, couldn't shut up about it, either. Too much talk can wreck a girl. Makes it easier to be tracked down, too—the real reason she eventually changed her name, keeping it separate for work. Ten years back, didn't she wither when the floppy-haired kid who'd been especially asking for her turned out to be her long-lost little brother? Half-brother. His wide eyes when she'd plopped onto his lap, grasping his buckle. He'd been a child when Sheila left, how was she supposed to know? He'd begged, then cried when she refused to go with him to the hostel to clean up before bussing back to that remote corner of the province. "You know how many women disappear? It's not too late," he'd said, sniffling. He'd held out the ticket, paid for by their mother, of all people. "Of course it's too late," she'd said back then.

Sometimes Sheila thinks she sees him in car windows, or on the bus, rolling past her corner. What would he look like now? She's changed a lot since; maybe he has, too. If he tracked her down again and waved another ticket in her face, would she go this time?

Maybe, maybe not.

What's home anyway? Her creepy stepdad's suburban split-ranch with the yellowed lawn and the German Shepherd short-chained out back? And her mother, mincing around, acting like he was such a great catch, the real deal, folding paper napkins under the short forks beside the frozen TV dinners, ginger ale poured out in plastic cups, while teenaged Sheila, seething, sketched and doodled inside her locked room? Or, before that, the bungalow near the lake, foggier in her mind, where she was born, where they lived with her dad before he took off, whenever that was.

Thinking backwards isn't good for the confidence and isn't good for business. Sheila's got to shake it off, get cranking. She stamps her feet back and forth on the hot asphalt.

Sheila is not fancy. She's getting old. But she still has nice legs, plus she's got experience, so let guys make up their own minds. She needs money, and they've got it. Look at them driving their big cars, of course they've got dough.

Ten, that'd be okay, plus a toonie for a donut. She loves the confetti sparkle ones. They only make them twice a year and there's three left on the shelf. That guy could save her one until she gets the coin together. It's not much to ask. That guy gets to have whatever he wants. She's seen him eat an egg-salad sandwich every day on break—half now and half later, wrapping the leftovers back up in the plastic and tucking them into the corner of the glass-front refrigerator. Plus he can probably have a confetti sparkle donut every time they make them. How is that fair? She'd owe him. She pays her debts. She pays her fucking rent.

Sheila high kicks across the intersection. More cars honking means more men noticing. Free advertising! Advertising takes a while to work. You hear the donut store jingle on the radio and you don't always want it right then. Sometimes it's the middle of the night before you realize you're a bit hungry, you forgot about dinner, you're actually starving and you need one *right now*. Same with pussy.

Sheila is good at self-promotion, no matter what Gord says. She knows her business. She's been doing it half her life. She'd like to see *him* out here working the corner. He'd have to clean up his act. He'd never make a cent. Bad teeth and breath like a dirty asshole, a deep funk to the old coat he never takes off. What does he know?

But never mind Gord, Sheila is doing okay. She is doing just fine. She is making her own artistic commercial for free, letting the guys know. She'll do her commercial now and take a heat break down at the air-conditioned Galleria Mall, stroll the hallway and check out the clearance bins, and maybe take a snooze in the mattress and furniture display, maybe drink a cup of that hotdog water they call coffee. Then later on, maybe even tonight after the concrete starts to cool and the night breeze shifts the humid air around, she'll be raking it in.

She'll be making a shitload one day.

Tracker & Flow

SEPTEMBER. Nineteen weeks in, Kelly's hard-won pregnancy is disrupted with news of an incompetent cervix. Tom sits in the chair beside her, nodding and rubbing her back while the doctor explains. Bed rest. Ovulation meds aside, she waited a bit too long to experiment with fertility, the doctor says. "Plus that scar tissue," he adds, frowning.

Through the open office door, down the deserted hall, a set of lights flicker. The doctor clicks his pen. He is waiting for Kelly to say something. Apologize? The initial ultrasound and pelvic X-ray were good, all things considered. She spent four grand on meds to stimulate egg production, five more to harvest and freeze the eggs themselves. Three hundred dollars a year, freezer rent while the supply dwindled. They're all used up now. She rests a palm on her rounded belly.

It isn't for lack of trying.

Twilight in the curtainless window behind the doctor's head—the office is closing. The doctor's family beams from a framed photo on his desk. He has a wife to go to, twin girls and a black poodle. Standard, not toy. Kelly shrugs Tom's hand away and stands, ready to leave.

Back at the condo Tom sits, one leg stretched to the cappuccino hemp rug, the other knee bent, balancing the remote pointed at the wide-screen TV: highlights for his fantasy hockey pool. Kelly calls the office, sends a dozen emails delegating work on her most pressing case. She'll miss most of the trial at this rate. It makes sense to give it to Angela and hope she doesn't screw up. Kelly eyes the open bottle of chardonnay, unstops it, sniffs and plugs it back up with the sterling top. She paces the length of the apartment until Tom swats her with the remote. She dusts a corner of the chrome coffee table with her bare hand. Kelly yanks open the tan and white vertical blinds and stands at the glass, looking out. The eighth floor is high enough for a view of the skyline, but not so high they can't handle the stairs if the elevators conk out. Down below, at this particular moment, a wild-haired panhandler is screeching and punching the windshield of a car trying to drive through the intersection. Property values in the neighbourhood are rising, albeit slowly. Kelly shuts the blinds and crosses the living room for the wine bottle. She pours the contents down the sink and slams the bottle in the recycling.

"I'll cancel dinner," she says.

"You still have to eat," he says.

"I'd rather order in."

"I've got kettleball, anyway."

Tom pats the couch beside him, but she looms in the doorway of the darkened nursery, formerly a study. It's like being backstage behind a closed curtain. All the props are set in place: miniature shelves neatly filled, mobile suspended, dollies standing at attention. She pulls the string on the dancing duck and a tinny version of Brahms' Lullaby begins to play. Beside the rocking chair is a stack of parenting magazines, dog-eared and cross-referenced, in which Tom has displayed zero interest. This baby will have only the best, she'll see to it. As the duck's legs slow their robotic jig and the music wanes, she can hear the panhandler's voice rising on the wind.

She doesn't cry. Not from the cramps, which wrench invisible female parts, or from lower back pain, which has her balled on the floor moaning. Not when burgundy clots bloom into the toilet bowl—uterine lining, placenta—and not even later, when she folds the tiny pastel stacks—bloomers and onesies and cheerful flannel squares. She keeps the crib, a family heirloom, but donates most of the other gifts. She begins feeding a young alley cat behind the condo and, one night, brings him inside.

"I'm allergic," says Tom.

"Don't be ridiculous," says Kelly.

She buys locally sourced, grain-free kibble, a silver comb, a rhinestone-studded collar. She posts photos of the cat online, sometimes dressed in the abandoned christening gown, sometimes wearing a beret. She can't possibly return to work, not yet. Her mother is worried. "Tom, *do* something," she hisses into the phone, loud enough so Kelly can hear. Friends call but Kelly doesn't want to talk. Angela is the worst. "Babies are for poor people, and parenting for the truly neglectful," she shouts before Kelly disconnects. The fertility clinic recommends a therapist—a sock and sandaled man who, within minutes of their first meeting, enquires about Kelly's relationship with her father. "Nice try, Freud," she says, and walks out.

Kelly shuns Tom, preferring the cat's sullen company. When Tom complains, sniffling and rubbing his eyes, Kelly buys a packet of Benadryl. He says the pills don't help. They slow his reaction time, however, and, like a zombie, he lurches for Kleenex, sneezing and trumpeting at all hours. When Tom works up the nerve to touch her, she flinches. Her body, sluggish and defeated, is off limits. Can't he see the cautionary tape, the neon pylons propped everywhere?

One night, she plays the duck's lullaby while swaddled, cat to breast in the rocking chair. Tom hovers in the doorway. "Kell, we should talk. Don't you think?"

"About your subpar swimmers?"

"W-we could try again," he stammers.

"We should have frozen embryos ten years ago," she says.

"Was that a thing, back then?"

Kelly turns from his pathetic wheezing and stares out the nursery window into the black. To hell with Tom, she should have used a sperm bank. She'd been tempted by the ginger special: redheads cost less. But people might have wondered.

Failure ruins things for Kelly; it gnaws her insides like a cancer.

Tom blows his nose and heads to bed without her.

October. The cat grows long and lean. Its front paws reach higher than the kitchen counter when it stands on hind legs, which it does frequently, sometimes taking several steps unaided. Its white fur coats everything they own, like insulation from a demolition, like asbestos. The cat enjoys crouching on top of the refrigerator or on the highest closet shelf and leaping out at the unsuspecting person, usually Tom, in feral ambush.

"We should get him neutered," sniffs Tom one morning, as the cat hunches on a pillow near his face. "Rat balls, look at the size of them!"

Kelly says, "No!" She kisses the pink nose tip, adding, "He's just a baby." When the cat shreds the upholstery on Kelly's designer couch, she says it doesn't matter. It rips the new bedroom curtains and digs up houseplants, leaving broken pots and clomps of soil throughout the condo, so Tom fills a spray bottle and spritzes it, once, right in the face. "Humane discipline," he says. "I googled it."

That night the cat pisses on Tom's side of the bed, while Tom is lying in it. He stuffs his reeking pyjamas into the washing machine and showers, but can't rouse Kelly to change the sheets. She took the insomnia medication again. The pills knock her out so completely that Tom sometimes checks for a pulse. The cat settles in beside her, purring. It looks smug, perhaps malevolent. Claws extend and retract across Kelly's cleavage. *Mine*, it seems to say. Tom can't remember the last time he touched Kelly's breasts. He misses them, like old college friends you don't see anymore, living a different kind of life in another city.

Tom gets a mothball-scented blanket from the closet and lies on the couch, shins dangling over the armrest. He'd amorously bent Kelly over that same armrest the night they moved in; they'd made love amidst the boxes, the suitcases. Now, springs push into his kidneys and he twists onto his side, trying to get comfortable. The cat dominates their home, no question. Just this week it broke the antique lamp, a vase filled with orchids—which it ate, then vomited into Tom's shoes—and three framed pieces of signed art, which shattered in piles on the floor. Tom has begun to wrap and box things away, all the knick-knacks, sugar skulls from their honeymoon in Mexico, anything delicate or of value. The cat watches his progress, batting at the roll of tape.

Kelly, at least, might be perceived as a desirable mate. But Tom has been pissed upon, the ultimate challenge—he read so online. *Unmanned*. Should've agreed to get a dog when she wanted one. He'd at least have an ally; dogs can be reasoned with. Those insufferable months of her canine campaign had shown him a new side of Kelly. He'd felt the brunt of her ire. She'd looked right through him when he asked about practicalities like *who would walk it* and *what kind of dog loved condo living.* "It would be home alone all day, every day," he said, and, "you'll expect me to do all the work." She shut him out completely, then. Like he was nothing. And when, in a desperate attempt to win back her affection, he began surfing the net for rescue dogs needing a forever home, she simply said, "No."

Tom can't get anything right lately. When pressed, the clinic nurse reveals his sperm samples averaged three million, which sounds like a lot to Tom, but Kelly hoped he'd be more like *fifteen* million. To spare his feelings the nurse says, "We're seeing a lot of this lately." Cell phones, pesticides, pot smoking, sweaty balls in too-tight pants—nobody knows why exactly, but Tom is definitely not pulling his weight in Project Baby. He's slacking off at the gym, starting to feel his age, and a slight paunch strains against his fitted shirts. Grey streaks have appeared at his temples, and each morning there are more hair strands wound around the bristles of his brush. When he flirts with the company intern, rather than laughing and blushing at his Top Forty jokes, she shrinks from him, eyebrows arched, and glossy lips puckering. There'd been a recent email about gender harassment, and he'd been made to watch a humiliating video about non-violence, *power-with* versus *power-over*, and emotional wellness in the workplace. As if he isn't a nice guy! And he was passed over for promotion when their biggest account switched to a rival phone company. He doesn't blame the clients. Not really.

Everyone wants a better deal.

Make yourself your first priority! Lavender and grey font with pink highlights. *You and Your Miscarriage* breaks information into small bits so even a distressed woman can process it. The bleeding stops more or less when it should, and Kelly's HCG levels are in steady decline. "A good thing," the nurse assures her. Kelly is supposed to take her temperature twice daily. A fever signals infection, which can lead to infertility. Kelly already knows this was a late last chance at forty-three. "Keep trying," urges the nurse, "you're not dead yet." But Kelly decides there'll be no baby, not now. With Tom's low count, and her endangered eggs, it is a humiliating, costly, uphill battle. She swipes her personal notes, an enormous case file, into the bin: twenty-five months of menstrual charts noting peak ovulation hours, optimum viscosity of mucosal discharge, body temperature, weight and mood shifts. Gone, too, the dozens of pregnancy and ovulation tests. No more peeing on sticks. Before this pregnancy she'd already had early perimenopausal symptoms—rage accompanying hot flashes and a propensity for misplacing nouns. She reads the pamphlet again and throws it out. Adoption is out of the question: someone else's castoff isn't the point. And she will not be joining a support group, forget it. Other suggestions include *journal about your journey* and, even less helpful, *pray*. Everyone warns about depression, especially Angela, who barges past Tom and his weak protests at their doorway.

"The concierge let me in," she says. She towers over Kelly in the rocking chair, wielding a bottle of Scotch. Angela wears dove-coloured Armani, plenty of filler, her forehead Botoxed to an impenetrable shine. "Frankly, you dodged a bullet, Kell. Think we made all this money just to pour it into a diaper service? At least we can have a bloody drink now. Tom, get some glasses."

Kelly glares at Tom, who simply shrugs. When he turns toward the mess of a kitchen, Angela says, "What, did you fire the maid?" And, seeing the pained look on Kelly's face says, "You want to micromanage a toy box for the next ten years?" In this light Kelly can see the line of Angela's foundation, not quite blended along the jaw. Why doesn't Kelly have any other female friends?

Angela regales her with office gossip in the hopes it will lure Kelly back to work—the receptionist has gone gay, *finally*; Mary in accounting, slammed with a DUI, has to give up her license.

"I'm quitting the firm," Kelly says when Angela finally stops talking.

"You're joking, right?"

Kelly watches the scene unfold. Tom, nearly dropping his glass. Angela gasping, eyes rolling madly at Tom.

"I'm tired," says Kelly. Picking up the cat, she shuffles into the darkened bedroom and shuts the door. She can hear Angela in the living room.

"Tom, what the hell."

Tom's nervous stutter. "This has been really t-tough on her."

Platitudes. Like he has nothing to do with any of it, like this is *her* thing. There's been no hysteria. Privately, she is relieved—this part of her life is over, and she only has to wait and see what's left of it to find out what will come next. Then she met the cat. Only the cat does not look at her with pity. Only the cat does not whisper or worry or expect much from her. It needs her and it does *not* need her. Its ambivalence is remarkably reassuring.

Kelly finds her pill bottle under the bedside table and, still on her knees, shakes two tablets into her palm. She swallows them with the rest of her Scotch. She dreams being twenty again: clueless, in debt, subletting a dirty room from strangers. Montreal in the early 1990s was like an acid trip at a carnival-themed after-hours bar. Men appear from her past, embarrassing ghosts. The insipid poet with the asymmetrical haircut, the dreadlocked actor who refused to bathe, and that rich, pretty one everyone thought was gay. After a casual coffee date, he had surprised her by performing intercourse with almost no warning in her front foyer, at an alarmingly fast pace and only partially disrobed; when she insisted on a condom he conceded, only to discreetly tug it off pre-release. Hence the first bewildering pregnancy and subsequent abortion, half of which was paid for by his mother via his weekly allowance. Goddamn little prince. Kelly had tamped this down, buried it—this and so many other indignities. Now, years later, she tries to speak up, but in her dopey dream state cannot. She strikes out again and again, slurring.

Then Tom is shouting, "Kelly, wake up! It's only me."

"Get out," she gasps, and he does.

He takes the smelly blanket and heads for his new lair, the dilapidated couch. When he closes the bedroom door, she begins to weep.

Tom is normally a laid-back guy. His response to being let go surprises everyone at the office, and security has to be called. "You want my keys?!" he screams, and throws them at the division manager's head. His severance package includes four months' salary, but they want him to sign a release. Tom hesitates, and the manager reveals that a formal complaint has been filed on behalf of the intern. There are multiple incidents *with* witnesses; it will get messy if Tom tries to fight. Tom insists the girl has misunderstood. He was only ever trying to be friendly!

Never much of a drinker, Tom amazes himself by marching across the street to the Irish pub. Three pints at the bar, a plate of crisps from a kilted redhead—she can hardly be old enough to serve him—a round of shots, his treat, after he shares his misfortune with the beautiful barmaid—she is young, yes, but a good listener, mature for her age—and the lumps on adjacent stools. He doesn't want to buy *them* a drink, but it looks better, less like a married man hitting on a pretty girl. Another round, a third and fourth—someone else is paying, he thinks—and later, much later, wallet empty and remaining tab paid on VISA, Tom is face in the toilet, bringing up all that alcohol, tie trailing through sick, face hot, stomach churning, kneeling in what just might be the smear of someone else's feces on the filthy bathroom floor. When he stumbles back out through the pub, everyone laughs.

Mid-afternoon: no one sits near him on the subway ride home. The concierge, impeccably discreet, ducks behind his desk, allowing Tom to stagger to the elevator in shame, for which Tom is grateful.

Inside the condo it is hot and putrid. *Cat shit.* The turd, alarmingly large and moist, glistens from the centre of the couch: Tom's new bed. He chokes on the fumes. The blinds are still drawn and breakfast dishes congeal in the sink, miserably. He staggers around the apartment. Kelly is nowhere. Then he identifies the silent lump under the duvet next to the cat, who looks right through him and, with great satisfaction, continues to groom.

Tom yanks the cord hard, raising the blinds, assaulting the room with sunshine. He drags the couch toward the screen door. Hauls it onto the balcony. It sticks out halfway and he pulls, swearing voraciously, losing a shoe. He summons his strength and, with another great heave, manages to pop the shitted-upon couch all the way through. The screen door jumps its tracking and clatters onto the cement balcony. "Fuckity fuck!" Tom balances the couch on the rail and shoves it over the edge with a violence that feeds his rage, just a bit. Under a clear blue sky he watches it fall, a sense of doom gathering in the pit of his gut. The sound, when it lands several storeys below, is satisfying. Like a gunshot, reverberating off the bricks, silencing everyone.

The living room now bare, the nursery is the only option. Tom lowers one side of the vintage crib, turning it into a kind of delicate day bed. He strips his clothes and throws them in a corner with his other shoe. If he curls tight enough, knees to chin, he can just fit.

November. Kelly lies in bed, trying to remember the first time she wanted *things*. Money or nice clothes or a car. She hadn't always been this way—griping about cappuccino foam to thirty-year-old baristas, or incensed that her preferred granite countertop was out of stock. She'd been a bohemian teen: tie-dyed scarves and sandalwood incense. She'd read poetry, played guitar badly. Shouted to save the rainforest. *No nukes!* She had threatened art school but somehow, law prevailed. In Montreal she'd seen enough young women flake out. She'd nearly been one of them, especially after the whole gay-not-gay boyfriend episode: day-drunk, smoking unfiltered Gauloises, eating crackers dry from the box. Underweight with irregular periods—there were no tracking apps back then—and yet she was so fertile, a nubile Aphrodite! She and every other girl spent so much energy trying to *not* get pregnant: a cruel joke. She'd felt hunted in that city, as though an invisible target was plastered over her uterus, drawing every scumbag to her when she walked the streets, or simply went about her daily life. Boyfriends hadn't protected her, only complicated things. Eventually Kelly chose to take care of herself.

She wills herself to sit. To shuffle into her slippers. The apartment is empty and not just because Tom is gone. There's more space, somehow. She peers about the nursery. Laundry on the floor, a foulness emanating from it. Tom is dispensing with all formalities. It takes her a moment to understand that the crib is demolished. The slats are broken, the sides collapsed, bars pointing every which way, like a broken ribcage.

She eases into the rocking chair and coos for the cat. He struts slowly, tail lifted, and stops two feet away. Kelly pats her lap. He blinks lazily. He should come. Why doesn't he? She saved him from a life of filth and danger, but he doesn't seem to care. Kelly is flabby and stiff at the same time; she stopped going to the gym. She never leaves the apartment anymore. Why bother? This city, looking out the floor-to-ceiling windows, is all dirty squares and rectangles. *Ugly*. Around her, the condo is unrecognizable. Bare walls, the bookcase thinned to empty, no more personal touches. All their nice things, gone. Tom wrapped them in protective paper, but even the wraps are chewed and shredded. Where is the couch?

The kitchen is a disgrace—grease-soaked pizza boxes tower beside the stove, which hasn't been used in weeks. Tom was so proud, choosing the retro 1950s-style gas range, fire-engine red, a nod to his brief stint in chef school back in the day. Kelly didn't feel like washing dishes, so she'd stopped using them. The bathrooms haven't been cleaned since it happened. They remind her of a roadside latrine she once used while honeymooning in Mexico.

In Mexico they had both gotten food poisoning and spent most of the time competing for the hotel toilet, sometimes puking into the shallow tub while, simultaneously, a diarrhoeic storm blew out the other end. Not the erotic adventure she'd planned. But they'd discovered a primal bond, the result of surviving adversity, like prison or military combat or a hostage-taking, she imagined.

When did she decide on a baby? It certainly wasn't Tom's idea: nothing is. Kelly and Angela used to joke about the self-described *yummy mummies* who swarmed the neighbourhood en masse: sleep-deprived, humourless, unsexed. White-knuckling their strollers. Jogging, for god's sake. Suckered, and for what?

Kelly's mother once said, "If you don't have children, who'll look after you when you're old?"

"Ha," laughed Kelly. "Who's looking after *you*?"

Now the question chafes.

Hormones working overtime, correcting past mistakes: these might help explain her change of heart. Truthfully, she was bored with their domestic routine, and less compelled at work. *Lonely*. It was the obvious next move, and Kelly simply set her mind to it. Like staying on the correct side of the road, keeping to the speed limit. Almost everyone does it. Once decided, she was resolute. She is losing one egg, a potential baby, every six to seven minutes.

Tick tock.

The cat stretches and yawns. He steps up, gingerly, and settles on top of her: front paws and face at her breast, belly to belly, breathing in time with her, haunches warming her wounded lap. The cat begins to purr.

"I told you we should have mounted it. Now look." Lines deepen around Kelly's disapproving mouth. Morning light reveals grey streaks in her thinning, unwashed hair. She toes a large black shard where it shines on the floor.

Tom is dehydrated and cannot rinse the foul taste of last night's vomit from his mouth. To cure his hangover, he tried to go for a run. A dry-heaving disaster. His head imploded. He is closer to crying than he's been in years. It had been a beautiful seventy-inch flat screen with state-of-the-art colour and definition. The cat sits on the console where the television once presided, licking a paw.

"I smell a poopy," says Kelly. "Did someone miss the litter box?"

Kelly hands him the broom and Tom brandishes it like a sword. He is overcome with an urge to strike the cat, to throw it over the balcony like he did the couch, this thing that is dismantling his life, piece by piece.

The cat growls and leaps. Tom raises an arm to protect his face—too late—claws slash it. Fangs latch into the flesh of his thigh. Tom chucks the broom and shakes off the beast, all three of them screaming, the cat pissing indiscriminately. Tom flees the apartment, howling, taking the stairs barefoot, two at a time, all the way down, bursting into the back alley. The door slams behind him.

There is his despicable couch, a carcass in the alley. Even the men from the homeless shelter next door won't sit on it, preferring to smoke on the curb. Pain and dizziness force Tom to lean on the green dumpster. He squats beside it, head between knees, breathing deeply. Blood soaks his Dockers. His leg throbs. Skin shrieks, heated and stinging, and he can't see out of his left eye; his face is swelling.

A man shouts, "His Magistrate, forsake me not!" Tom recognizes the voice as one that frequently wakes him during the night, shout-singing at top volume. Condo residents regularly complain about *The Duke*. He wears a cardboard Burger King crown and over-sized bathrobe, the hem of which drags through the dirt as he marches. Tall and slim, he possesses a kind of regal carriage that surprises Tom.

The Duke strides toward Tom and peers close. "You don't smell too good, mister," he says, backing away. "His Magistrate!"

Tom scowls.

Their lives—Kelly's, but mainly his—have descended into chaos. In truth it's one of the reasons he never wanted children. All that mess. After Kelly miscarried, Tom proposed another trip. "Not Mexico," he said. "Costa Rica?" They needed intimacy. Time, of course, and eventually sex. Sex without this unnerving scientific goal of impregnation, three pre-determined days each month. Like Mormons, he thought. Early on, he and Kelly used to experiment with role-playing, costumes, battery-operated implements. Cocaine and the occasional threesome. It was Kelly's daring approach to sex—surprising him in heeled boots and a leather harness, tying his wrists tightly and fitting his mouth with the orange ball gag—that hooked him. He dropped the other women he'd been dating and fell into Kelly's open palm, incredulous.

Now she's just distant and mean. If he tries to kiss her, the tickle of whisker intervenes. "He's jealous," Kelly says, pushing Tom away. The cat literally comes between them, extinguishing all spark of possibility. Tom doesn't even want sex anymore. He isn't at his best. Neither is she, shuffling around in fusty pyjamas. Her slippers, in particular, keen a lonesome song, flattened to unremarkable grey, loose soles slapping the floorboards.

Still, it isn't her fault. She needs support. They said so at the clinic, the one time he accompanied her. And, unlike Tom, she isn't used to not getting her way. Normally Kelly sets her course and triumphs. It's the thing that drew him to her so long ago. Without Kelly, he'll have to start over. Work a whole lot harder. He's been coasting, relying on her for years, and it never once occurred to him that she could falter. Terrifying! Self-awareness in a lightning bolt: he is an aging, unemployed creep with a lamentable sperm count. The deck is stacked. Who else would have him?

He shivers in the bitter cold.

He should go back up. Make amends.

It's hard to get on his feet. Tom has to pull himself up using the dumpster. He can't put weight on his wounded leg, which is still bleeding. Drops ooze down it, pooling and drying on his dirty foot. He's read about cat bites, that they're notoriously brutal. The wounds he can see are raised, red, and hot to touch. He's sweating and also chilled: already infected. He hops toward the back door, braces himself against a rising wind using the brick wall for balance. He pats his pockets, front and back, for his keys.

He left them upstairs.

The sky turns.

It takes the better part of an hour to hobble around the building to the front entrance. Tom sways and nearly collapses waiting for Kelly to buzz him in. Rain, then sleet, pelt him. No answer. Probably back in bed. Dust and litter and empty plastic bags gust past. Tom waves frantically at the concierge, who threatens to call the police.

"It's me," he shouts, to no avail. He catches his reflection in the front window—unkempt, face bloodied and swollen beyond recognition. Tom wouldn't let himself in, either.

Kelly wraps herself in a shawl and stares out at the storm. Wind batters the folding chairs on the balcony. Hail drills the glass. Tom doesn't come home. Is there someone else? She wouldn't put it past Angela to scoop him. He's handsome and fairly fit. Easygoing but headed towards sloppy. Losing his edge, like so many. Few men grow more potent with age, honing charm and style. Tom is still a decent catch—manageable, but with a spark. He doesn't dominate; he likes her taking the reins. Objectively, neither one of them is very nice, but they complement each other. If only he could stand by her now, when she's floundering.

Kelly hasn't really *looked* at Tom in a long time. Even before the pregnancy, which she can see was a last-ditch effort to infuse their relationship with purpose. Children would give them an all-consuming past-time. They'd be a team again, Team Family. Otherwise, what? Long distance running? Swinger parties? Kelly needs focus, momentum, control, and Tom needs direction. Without them, things unravel.

When Kelly was a teenager and learning to drive, her hands sweated, her jaw clenched; her body would be stiff with fear. She had to consciously fight the urge to crank the wheel towards an oncoming vehicle or into the deep ditch that lined the rural roads, every time she climbed into the car. She obsessed: one false move and she'd wind up killing everyone. *Head games*. Eventually, she learned how to flick the mental switch and get on with driving, with living. Since the miscarriage, she's become that lost girl again, anxious and unhinged. How far will she let herself fall?

Kelly is on the cusp of some radical thinking, and to quell that discomfort she reaches for the pill bottle. Nearly empty. She shakes out the last tablets and soon she's underwater again, slogged and toppled. Limbs become tentacles, curling, uncurling. Such exquisite submission. She is dreaming again, falling down a manhole into the sewer. Then she's clawing her way back up, fingernails breaking. Soil filling her mouth, so no screaming. Flailing in muck, the cruddy dregs swamping her.

Noises pierce her shadow world.

Ringing. More ringing.

The weight of the cat pinning her, paws on her shoulders, paws on her bladder, yowling in her face.

Alarm sounding. Smoke.

Kelly ties her bathrobe, finds her slippers. She cradles the cat and braves the hazy living room.

Fire lights the kitchen: flames, from the stack of pizza boxes.

Later she will wonder why she didn't reach for the extinguisher or disconnect the gas line. Save the condo, or at least their part of the building? The pills, her panic, the deafening alarm—the cat leaps and she chases him instead.

"Cat!"

She corners him in the nursery; lifts him, hissing, into trembling arms. In the hall, the building alarms are also shrieking. Heads poke out of doorways and, seeing smoke, neighbours begin to hustle. The cat is tense, gripping her forearms. Down the stairs she rushes. It is dizzying, all that white paint, the bright lights, the staircase's tight turns.

Outside in the post-storm freeze, the trucks arrive, clanging and honking and blocking the intersection. They're getting hoses out and opening hydrants. Residents huddle in the back alley, several with leashed dogs or small pet carriers. No children, not in this building. Young professionals and a few retirees mingle with homeless men from next door. Nobody approaches Kelly, who's clutching the cat, forlorn. She becomes aware of her greasy hair, her grubby nightshirt and bathrobe, her tattered slippers. When did she last bathe? She hasn't been outside in weeks. The frigid air, although darkening with ash, buoys her.

A sound like an engine backfiring provokes startled gasps from the crowd. Black clouds spew out the windows of her beautiful condo and golden flames lash the balcony. Kelly tilts her head back to see. The cat is sniffing the air and his tail swats back and forth the way it does when he's hunting moths inside. He struggles.

"His Magistrate!" The Duke careens toward Kelly, arms outstretched.

The cat's claws dig in. He launches from her forearms and leaps for the older man.

"Reunited at last!" says The Duke, and he and the cat bump foreheads. The cat sniffs the man's mouth and climbs onto his shoulders, where he settles, purring and kneading his bathrobe, like some living, consenting fur collar.

"You stole His Magistrate," he says to Kelly.

"He was out here all alone," she says.

The man shakes his head. From his shoulders, the cat stares—pitiless, but relaxed, despite the chaos of the moment. The Duke saunters down the lane. His Magistrate blinks once before they turn the corner.

Kelly's lips move, no sounds. Her arms hang at her sides, empty.

Sitting apart from the gathering crowd on what looks like Kelly's old couch, is a roughed up transient with a blackened eye and unclean wounds. He stands up, wavering.

Impossible.

Soaked through. Barefoot and bleeding, red shiny skin swollen to bursting. Feverish, one-eyed.

Tom: stripped bare.

"Kell, you're safe." He limps toward her.

He's still *here*.

"I've been a complete ass," he says, eyes watering.

Kelly tightens the belt of her robe. There is a piece of gravel inside her slipper, cutting into the arch of her foot. She hasn't thought about *her foot* in months, not since her last pedicure. Snowflakes drift, fat lacy miracles, onto her eyelids, her lips. Tom reaches out his hand, dirt-caked and broken-nailed, and Kelly holds on.

Affliction: The Taming of Bloor West West

White white, they glow
Squeak slide, they flow
Now they're on his feet he can never let them go:
Second-hand sneakers from the Value Village clearance row

JIMMY sashays the Value Village parking lot wearing the stolen sneakers. He moonwalks next door, to Club Paradise Gentlemen's Lounge on Bloor Street West. Shimmies past the front door and twirls down Strippers' Alley, where two Club Paradise dancers have popped out the side door for a smoke. He points to his feet. "Look at my new shoes." They go, "Nice one, Jimmy." He shuffle-steps. He ball-changes. He grapevines, waggles his jazz hands and bows. One girl tosses a toonie. "Thank you kindly," he says, tucking it into his change purse. They say, "Dance with us inside," and he says, "Regretfully, I must decline. Too many electronics in there, ladies. That's how they track you."

Beside the gentlemen's club is Bethlehem Apostles United, and the service is in full swing. The choir is bursting out the roof beams, *Lord is King*. A sign says *Free Coffee for a Prayer*, but Jimmy doesn't pray for coffee. Jimmy *pays* for coffee. He marches past the church, past the Bank of Montreal, where the teller sits inside, yawning, flicking her nails. Jimmy tippity-taps his feet while he waits on the corner for the light to turn green, for the little white man to say *walk*.

"Lift left. Lift right. Lift left, right, left!"

Jimmy marches across four lanes, past the cars and the cyclists and the baby mommas' strollers. He parks it in front of the donut shop on the other side of Lansdowne and Bloor. Puts his hand out, puts his hat on the ground, does a little soft-shoe, does a little stomp. "Your coins are much appreciated," he says to the people streaming past. A blonde lady with twin bald babies hides her leather purse. Joggers hurdle the hat. "Neon wants to dance," says Jimmy, "but spandex got to go go go!" Jimmy does the Watusi. Does the Hippy Hippy Shake. He does the Mashed Potato. "Your coins are much appreciated," he says, and dabs his brow with a paper napkin that he pulls from his pants pocket.

The hat is still empty.

When no one is looking, he takes the stripper's toonie from the change purse pinned to the inside of his brown suit jacket. He tosses it in the hat.

Encouragement for the People.

Jimmy sings, "Knees up, Mother Brown, swing your arms round and round." He gyrates his hips. "Your coins are much appreciated." He hears the clink of loose change falling into his hat. "Thank you, sir." More clinks. "Thank you, ma'am." There's a downright maelstrom of tin orchestration. But it's not coinage, no! It's Birdie's busted shopping cart piled high with beer tins and empty bottles, careening down the street. Garbage day! Birdie's doing real good. She drops a dollar in the hat (she owes him ten).

Jimmy says, "Thank you, Birdie."

Birdie says, "Jimmy can dance. Jimmy sure can dance."

He loosens his collar and mops perspiration from his hairline, from the back of his neck. The napkin is sopped and used right up. Jimmy keeps dancing. He does the hula. Fingers mime the ocean, palm trees, a tropical breeze. He licks his lips. He sure could go for an iced tea. He'd like to take a break but the shoes keep shuffling back and forth, back and forth. Bewitched. There's no stopping them. Whose were they anyway—M.J.'s?

Three skinny girls with too much makeup and not enough skirt jitterbug out the donut shop door, stab pink mouths with cigarettes, snap a lighter underneath—once, twice, shake it good. Spark a light and suck suck suck. Blow smoke out their noses, out the gaps of their chipped teeth.

Jimmy coughs and waves the smoke with flailing arms.

"Heya Pops," says one. "You feelin' good? What you got?"

Jimmy says, "Don't step on my hat."

She lifts her tiny wrists, shakes her hair. Thrusts her bony ass at him.

"Stop that, now," he says. "Behave." Licks his lips again. Can't catch his breath.

Car honk. Teenaged boys swarm the corner. The tallest flashes a twenty. The shortest sticks out his rear and flaps his arms. Puts his ball cap on the ground.

Jimmy says, "Go on, get. This is my corner!"

The kid gargles, "Go on, get."

Imitating Jimmy!

No respect.

The girls laugh, crook fingers at the boys, consider the twenty-dollar bill, ask what else they got? They are jutting hips, flipping crow-black hair. Boys hunch, shove hands deep into pockets, look at the ground, not at each other. Tall boy flashes a small pipe and the girls nod *yes*. Boys buzz. They all cross the street, past the bank, past Bethlehem Apostle. They duck into Strippers' Alley together.

Jimmy's got his corner back. Now he can really pull some shapes. He's winded. But his feet keep skedaddling, can't stop them no how. The shoes tighten on his feet. He bends down to unlace them but the strings are knotted, confounding him. Tries to pry them off but his feet are jammed in tight, glued. Can't pull these kickers off his swollen dogs.

Jimmy cannot stop dancing.

By God these shoes are hexed!

He checks his hat—his two dollars are gone!

"Hey!"

Darlene comes out of the donut shop wearing a straw-brimmed hat with dozens of yellow chicks sewn onto it. Get them for five cents at Easter. Her belt is a plastic inflatable pool toy—the giraffe head bounces against her chest. It stares at Jimmy with God-blue eyes and girl-length lashes.

Jimmy says, "Looking good, Darlene."

"Don't touch me," she says, slapping his shoulder.

Her hand fuses to Jimmy's suit jacket. She pulls, pulls, but can't release.

Jimmy shrugs and shakes. She flops like a ragdoll. "Let go," she shouts, and he says, "Now, wait a minute, Darlene."

Jimmy steps away. Darlene stumbles behind. Jimmy grabs his hat and stuffs his bald head into it. She bends and swoops with him. He leaps to the left. She tumbles along, screeching. Harley, her sometime boyfriend, barges out the donut shop door yelling, "Get back here, Darlene!" He grabs her neck. Jimmy jumps again. Now both of them clatter along. A car honks; people stare.

"I believe we have adhered," says Jimmy. More sweat in his open collar.

Those girls and the guilt-faced boys pour back out the alley onto Bloor Street. Boys swagger. Girls pop mints and hustle to Jimmy's corner on a yellow light. The one that danced with him says, "Still at it, pops?" She pinches his cheek. "Don't," he says, but it's too late. That skinny hen is affixed to his flesh. Her friends yank, and they become linked. Gasping, tug o' warring, like on some two-bit variety show.

Darlene gurgles with Harley's paw on her throat. Darlene's mom busts outside with her bedazzled walker. She whacks Harley with her alligator purse. She's stuck, too. Her new man punches Harley—now he's glued. Birdie's back, ramming her shopping cart into the mix. Each time an empty can tinkles to the ground she says, "That's five cents!" Lisa G's coffee scalds Harley's backside. "Faawk," he squeals, and tries to take a swing. They are bulging over the curb; they are becoming a spectacle.

The bells ring and, across the street, Bethlehem Apostle lets out. The congregation advances: purses swing, bonnets tilt, the Lord's light falls on still-humming lips. They wear brushed suits with hemmed pantlegs, flowered dresses. The stoplight changes, here they come! They're crossing over. Heading this way, pushing through Jimmy's crowd.

"Mercy!"

"What in the—"

"Off my foot, sister!"

Mrs. Morris swats the girls with her personally engraved bible. Mrs. Morris adheres. She shouts, "Stanley! Do something!" Her husband's eyes bulge. He's latched on, too.

Lisa G. shouts, "Help!"

Jimmy's spellbound shoes are bringing the People together. The sneakers have come with a greater purpose.

He says, "United, we face a common enemy."

He says, "United, we move as one!"

The squirming, fretting crowd has no choice but follow.

Jimmy pirouettes to the convenience store, where Mickey sells DKs and Sago under the counter. Cha-chas past Ali Baba's: it's two-falafel Tuesday. Congas along the dirty sidewalk past the anarchist bike shop. Collects the sallow, bearded youth who hang out front. Jimmy's mob is growing; it's kicking up dust. Girls stumble and shriek. Darlene moans and Harley keeps squealing, "Faawk!" Mrs. Morris weeps, "Forgive me, Jesus!" Past the nefarious shooting gallery, the boarded-up storefronts, the nutbar yuppie health shop, the ten-dollar barber, the Happy Cup Chinese Buffet, the hot-pink South Indian Dosa, right on down to Duffy's Tavern, open since 1949.

Out front, Bugsy paces the sidewalk. He's got a baseball bat and he wants to use it. He says, "What're you doing with my girls, Jimmy?"

Jimmy says, "Those skinnies?"

He says, "That's right."

"Bugsy, I'll trade the girls for that bat."

He says, "No way."

"All right," says Jimmy, and grabs the bat with two strong hands. Bugsy is taller, bigger, meaner, but Jimmy has conviction: he's on a mission. Jimmy flicks Bugsy to the left and his girls smother him, wailing. Bugsy yells, "You're dead meat, Jimmy."

Jimmy does the Stroll. Does the Worm. Drags this pack of sorry souls another half block to Bengali Grocery: *We Unlock Cell Phones, We Buy Your Gold*. He stops in front of Ernie's TV & Appliance. Nemesis! Inside the big front window, televisions blaze floor to ceiling. "People! I believe we have been brought here for a reason," he says. "Today we take a stand against the Electronic Kingdom. A pox on these brain-drainers!"

"Not this again," says Darlene.

Jimmy says, "People! This is *our* day. Watch me now!"

"Jimmy, don't."

"He's crazy. Stop him!"

Fingers on the bat. By God, his grip is good. Jimmy's better than a young man, he's got experience, can't lay him down. Bend and shake his tail feathers. He says, "Sss-trike one. Sss-trike two. Batter, batter, batter, sssa-wing. Got me a homerun!" Glass breaches to the break. Crickle-crack, lines ferret the nameplate. A thousand shards drop like cymbals. Split and shatter like a nice hi-hat. Glass rains down, percussion. Alarms begin to clang. Lights flash. Electric Circus!

People shriek, "Help. Help!"

Jimmy shouts, "Ladies and Germs! Step inside, watch the glass. Step inside this place, where evil is begot." Jimmy clears shards with his magic shoes. Inside, a hundred televisions hypnotize: walls of colour and noise. He says, "Talking boxes! Controlling your minds and you don't even know it!"

"Shut up, schizo," says Darlene.

He says, "Corrupting America. Pulverizing the creative mind, stupefying the Nation!"

He says, "It's the news. It's football, it's a soap opera. Telling you how to live. Telling you what to buy."

"Lunatic," shouts Bugsy's girl.

He says, "Take the chip out of your head, sever the cord, free yourselves. You know what to do, People. Deliverance is thine!"

Jimmy flings his limbs and the people fly off him, land in piles on the wall-to-wall shag carpet. People roll and moan. Scramble and climb. Pet their wounds. Swarm Ernie's aisles, fifty ants on a cookie crumb.

"Suckers," Jimmy shouts.

"Suckers," he hoots.

Little tiara-wearing white girls strut across a screen. Jimmy dances for the box hostages, for the children of the night. *Bomp, da da dah. Bomp, da da dah!* He says, "Poor little biddies try too hard. Me, I'm Solid Gold!"

Jimmy swings the bat. He wiggity-whacks a newsman.

Swings the bat. Hits the boy band.

Swings the bat. Hits the rednecks.

Get up offa that thing, huh.

Harley hauls a wide-screen, he's gone. Mrs. Morris tucks a blender to her bosom. Hipsters pour through the broken window. Maybe a hundred, maybe more. But they don't *kill* the box. They *covet* the box. Gather and cradle them. Take whatever they can. Lisa G. is crying, someone is bleeding. Still they grab and grab.

"No, People," says Jimmy. "You got the wrong number."

Fistfight among the air poppers. Darlene's mom reaches for a microwave. She's gonna fight Mrs. Morris for it; that woman's got girth.

Shadows. Heads duck, hands jab. Colours swirl, sirens whirl.

Someone yells, "Five-oh! Five-oh!"

Popsicle rockets spin, red-white-blue, pull up outside, *woop woop.*

"Cops!"

Bugsy dumps Birdie's shopping cart, bottles and tins everywhere. He sings, "Kill the policeman, blaat blaat. Kill him, kill him dead now. Blaat blaat!" Bugsy throws merch and his skinny girls fill the cart. They got a system: teamwork.

Jimmy says, "People!"

Tok, tok, tok, tok. Uniforms line up outside the broken window.

Shields flip up.

Batons *thump, thump* the shields.

Tok, tok, tok, tok. Thump, thump.

Tok, tok, tok, tok. Thump, thump.

That bass line really shakes it.

Jimmy catches Lisa G. Wild eyes, breath fogging him, she's sweating deep fryer from the Dosa shop.

"Let me go," she cries. "Cops!"

He says, "Fuck television. Fuck the police. Dance with me."

But Lisa can't stop crying and Jimmy, sadly, yields. "You, my dear, are exonerated."

Lisa uproots in the people current, surfs arms and legs, tows downriver in that stink of desperation. The bearded boys, those hipsters sucked under, get danced upon, crushed, but not Lisa. She rides the high-tide bottleneck to the back door, where an emergency axe lands once, twice: The People want out. Curling wave pulls flesh height, body weight, snuffs oxygen and light. Moans shrink to silence. Then, whoosh—the alley door busts outward, bodies rush, the tumble of injured life, plastics, electronics. Limbs paddle and slide, wrestle boxes and styrofoam chips. Let flow this river of discontent!

Jimmy's got his dance floor back, now he's really got some space.

Feet wanna hop, hips gotta drop!

Swings the bat. Hits the talk show. Crunches glass with his voodoo shoes. Primal, this hot wet drum love, this ritual cleanse.

"This is substance, People! What it is."

Hums a thrum bullfrog-deep in his throat, *yeah.*

Tok, tok, tok, tok. Thump, thump.

Gunfire: *Blaat Blaat.*

Megaphone: *Put your hands up, your hands up!*

Jimmy drops the bat. Raises his hands. Swings his hips, *yeah yeah*, they like that.

Blaat blaat.

Last Call at the Dogwater Inn

FIRST, there is Jimmy's six-pack of O.V., warm and bereft. I keep it company, washing down a handful of prescription pills from his bedside table. Jimmy's door is open and the afternoon sun is a lake of fire drawing and curling and surging to smite me as I perch on the edge of his bed. All the motel rooms are laid out similarly, but Jimmy's smells like shoe polish and mothballs and faint traces of diarrhea. Like denture powder and Old Spice cologne. Like a man who lived and died alone.

Inside the tiny bedside drawer is a well-thumbed pocket bible, St James edition. A pair of dollar store reading glasses. Round white candies that may have once tasted like mint. Swaddled in a handkerchief is a feather, probably pigeon, like a time-sanded relic from the Holy crèche. Scraps of paper penned in his furtive scrawl say, *St Barbara among the heathens!* And, *Cripple Civilian Society—Villains!*

I wouldn't exactly call it living, but I've been next door three years, ever since Delia chased me out of Detroit, back to my side of the border. I rarely set foot in Jimmy's room. It is void of many niceties. Obviously, no television; the man railed against them. No computers or electronics of any kind.

"Ray," he'd say, pointing at my bedside radio, "That's how they track you." And he'd lower his hat to deflect the lobotomizing frequencies. He often shout-sang to ward off evil as he paced up and down the block, fists at his side or threatening the sky: *Bop wop a doo-dah, bop wop yeah!*

Jimmy deranged me at first, all that humming and tapping, those scat vocals puncturing the thin wall between us. I was not at my best. I'd paid a week's rent, cash. Locked myself in that room on the tail of a lethal bender, heartsick and determined to end it all, but, miracle, I survived the unconscionable mix of dope and pills and bourbon and poison I'd brought with me. *Addict loser no-good asshole.* Delia's accusations drummed down on my wretched remains like a flash flood, a summer rainstorm with brimstone and thunder and bolts of lightning that zapped my last tender spots, killing them, but not the rest of me.

Plan B—forcible detox, since I couldn't walk, had no telephone, knew no dealers in this part of town. If I died, at least I'd have succeeded with the original plan. I lay cramped, sweating. When my bunged-up bowels finally moved, I shat myself profusely and couldn't crawl to the shower. Worms writhed my skin. I was beset by demons, which I later attributed to Jimmy's incessant, singsong voice, his abrupt barking and jazz hacks. Hours, maybe a day later, dragged along the crumbling balcony, I pounded his door, yelling, "Hie thee, Satan!" Jimmy opened a chained inch and said, "The government send you?" Which struck me as hilarious—that the government might send a shit-stained, detoxing maniac as a reliable representative. Jimmy unlocked and slipped me a lifesaving can of warm beer—O.V, always O.V.—which I shotgunned, and, instead of bashing his head in as I'd imagined, we became friends.

I rock back on Jimmy's cot, plastic creaking under the polyester coverlet. Roaches scurry to the corner. "They deserve a life, too," he'd say. A piece of foolscap taped high on his wall announces: *Do not impeach Biggie Smalls!* Jimmy alone campaigned on Biggie's behalf during a recent mayoral race that involved evangelical street-shouting and hand-written placards. (She got seventeen votes.) The candidate never once appeared in public.

Whenever I made crass jokes Jimmy would say, "Biggie Smalls and I cannot abide ignorance, Ray." One afternoon he said, "Biggie and I are heading to the beach, care to join us?" As Jimmy and I sauntered toward the lake, I wondered aloud, "Will we meet Biggie there?" "Ray," he said, "Biggie is with me wherever I go, unless she is breeding or feeding or otherwise feeling poorly." Jimmy spoke intimately to the crook of his arm and, later, into the depths of his coat pocket. He turned his head to listen for Biggie's response. Biggie, I assumed, was an imaginary slice of Jimmy's scrambled pie.

Stirring in a dim alcove above the note crouches the largest wolf spider I've ever seen; magnificent, furry, and somewhat familiar. A flash—me, drunk at the bar, and Jimmy lifting a palm-sized thing to his face adoringly. At the time I thought it was a hairpiece. Another hazed memory—me, collapsed on the rug in my room while Jimmy dances endlessly to a song I can't hear, his right hand extended for balance, his feet lifting and clopping, one-two, one-two, a furred lump creeping along his shoulders. *Biggie Smalls, straight outta the Georgia Woods*, Jimmy screeched.

Could it be? This, *this* is Jimmy's friend? Biggie Smalls in all her webbed glory, who will crusade for her now? A toast to Jimmy and Biggie is in order. I don't speak, just hoist the tin of beer.

Shadows fall upon me. Neilson, that rural numskull, appears in the sunsoaked doorway with a sickly little hustler. I'm not one to judge, but.

"Heard about Jimmy," says Neilson, and removes his hat.

I nod.

The hustler freezes like a hare and peers through dirty bangs at the ground.

"Come to pay respects," says Neilson, bathed in embers blown to flame.

"Door's open," I say, and that scares him. He'd rather a punch to the gut, that anti-social wolf.

Shadows liven their golden faces. Voices. I recognize Darlene's. She says, "I can't believe it. Just can't believe it!"

Darlene's mom rams her bedazzled walker past Neilson, makes straight for the only chair, and sits, heavily. Dust puffs out from around her rear end. Her entourage follows, crowding Neilson and his street trade away. The door pulls mostly closed and a dullness rides the room. It's cooler but gloomy. I blink to rid myself of red coals that shoot behind my eyelids. Now it's me and Darlene and her mom and the manager's niece, a glue-huffer whose name I don't know. Darlene is wearing something shiny around her neck, a wide collar, possibly made from aluminum foil. Her earrings are dangling styrofoam balls.

I feel woozy. The room closes in.

"Isn't it terrible, Ray? Just terrible," says Darlene's mom.

"We seen the cops leave, so we come up," says Darlene.

I succumb to Jimmy's flat, discoloured pillow. My jaw relaxes; saliva pools in my mouth. It takes all my strength to lift each leg and stretch it the length of the mattress. How many pills did I take?

"Darlene, see what he's got in the kitchen," says her mom. "I'm peckish."

My vision obscures to a blurred wash-out. I hear but cannot see Darlene wander off the carpet onto the linoleum, humming. The cupboard hinges quibble when she forces them. I feel each pressed-board slam in my marrow.

"Lipton Cup-o-Soup," Darlene shouts. "Saltines from the diner!"

"I'll take crackers," says her mom, and then the violence of her press-on nails tackling the plastic wrap. Crackling and crumpling and, finally, the seismic rupture. She crunches. Slurps. Stops to pick masticated lumps from her molars.

I cover my ears, whimpering.

The huffer darts and her hand closes over the pill bottle beside me, shaking it.

"Leave it," I mumble.

She unscrews the lid and peers inside. "Oxy, oxy, no oxy," she says, and sets it back down. Her face looms; eyebrows kneel in the centre of her lined forehead, her beak poised to stab.

"Gone," I whisper, and her eyebrows broaden and sink with despair.

Daryl's postnasal drip alerts me to the fact he has joined us and still has a baggie on him—the incessant tapping of fingers on that same pants pocket. Like my mother worrying her rosary, God in her skirt. Daryl has brought his dog. I can smell her dogginess, not unpleasant, not compared to the rest of the room and its occupants. She sniffs my bare toes, whiskery lick, presses her moist nose and snorts. *Shangri-La!*

More resident miscreants arrive to say farewell and snoop Jimmy's stuff. It's getting crowded and that anxiety-prone beast nurtures a quiet whine in the back of her throat. The jingle of her expired tags tracks the spin of her muzzle from Daryl's jerking movements to the rest of the unpredictable bipeds, back to her tweaked-out master. She turns a quick circle then scrabbles under the bed.

"Ray, Ray, you know Jimmy?" says Murray, the halfwit who lives with his mother in two-oh-seven. He passes a bottle. I slug off it. Sour mash.

"Cops shot him," Murray says, "then they tasered him."

"Domestic terrorism," says Mary Louise, his lesbian sidekick, the rockabilly butch.

"As if," sniffs Daryl.

Jimmy's voice haunts—*Let it be a lesson to any opposing the Western corporate regime: fast food, auto-oil, the Godwars!*

"To Jimmy," says Mary Louise.

"To Jimmy," we mumble. A clinking of bottles, the popping of beer-tin tabs, the rush and fizz of foam. Slurps. A few tears are shed. Darlene and her mom and the girl were there when it happened, been laying low ever since. They talk the most in order to quash their guilt about the loot they scored at Ernie's TV and Appliance, three blocks east on Bloor, where Jimmy took his last stand. Where Jimmy incited an actual riot in his perpetual war against electronics.

Tear gas! A shootout! Bender or no bender, how had I missed this?

An impromptu service of the funereal kind begins, and I would gladly desert, but those pills have kicked in and I have no control whatsoever over my limbs. I hope they're still attached to my torso, which rises higher, higher, floating near the stained ceiling squares. Hovering, I see it all: my body splayed on the cot, mourners encircling me, hungry for one last piece of the dead man.

Voices lift from the knot of bodies a galaxy away. Darlene's mom says, "Remember the time he hijacked the main office because the tax man was onto him?"

"Ha, that was funny."

"Was not, they held our cheques for three weeks," says Darlene.

Murray says, "We were on the news. On the TV!"

"Nearly gave him a stroke."

True. Acting out his beliefs, Jimmy was captured in photos and write-ups in the local paper, which only confirmed his suspicions. He'd say, "They're spying on me, Ray, I knew it!"

Everyone feels pretty bad for Jimmy, though I also feel bad for myself. The last drug-addled jazzman on the planet to give a shit about me, gone.

I descend back to my body, re-inhabit it. Jimmy's scent is in my nose, my hair. Lying where he slept each night, decked out in an open coffin, that's me, a spectacle. Friendless. I may as well *be* him, although I am white, debatably less crazy, and at least two decades his junior. Now I seep the lumpy mattress, drip through rusted springs, and puddle onto the dog shivering on the filthy carpet below. I burrow deep beneath the floorboards, the concrete sub-basement, into the ravenous, wormy earth.

Take, eat, this is my body.

Above me, Jimmy's other things are shared out amongst the neediest, the loneliest. Everyone claims a memento. Housecoat, slippers, good suit, a fine hat wrapped in tissue paper and stored in an old-timey box. A cardigan with mismatched buttons. His checkerboard. The sum of a man—is this it?

I'm not too proud to accept his ancient record player, which someone lowers sombrely onto my stomach. The weight of it propels me back from earth's bowels and up into my flesh. I sold off my vinyl eons ago but can keep an eye out. Used to find records at the end of each street on garbage day—people couldn't wait to junk them when they bought CD players. Now everyone tosses CDs. What next?

Daryl says, "He's in a better place now."

Darlene says, "The morgue? Won't someone have to get him?"

"He has a daughter," says Mary Louise.

"Huh."

I cannot begin to describe how the police dragged Ernestine, the muttering manager with the large ring of mislabelled keys, from her untidy office. How I crept from bed and peered out the eyehole. Who wants to see a broad expanse of uniform and badge first thing? Not me, but I hid my gear and stumbled into pants, a shirt I buttoned haphazardly, a jacket to cover the bruising along my inner arms. Barefoot, I opened up to bid them good morning.

"Afternoon," said the pink-complected ginger cop.

Ernestine eventually cracked Jimmy's door, and while the police searched the premises, she told me they'd shot him. Sixteen times. She said, "The daughter was sick of getting calls, so he put you down for emergencies. I been knocking since yesterday."

"What day was that," I asked, and she sucked her teeth.

"Raymond Jacobs?" The blonde cop rustled papers and pointed to sign, "Here and here. Oh and here."

"We're holding his things pending investigation," he said. "S.I.U."

The itemized list includes: one wallet (worn soft as a seal; I know it like my own); one leather belt (frayed at the end and notched tight to tie off with); one pair white sneakers (splattered red in my mind); one shirt; one pair pants; two dress socks; boxers; one brown fedora. Clothes no doubt folded stiff with blood.

"What about the bullets?" I said, and had to repeat myself since twat cops never listen.

"The sixteen bullets. They belong to him now? You gonna put them in the bag too?"

Gingersnap ignored me, but the blonde had the decency to blush when he said, "I don't think so."

"He never hurt a fly," I said, and my voice trembled. I pressed a fist to my lips to stop the rush of what had swum up my throat from my churning wet belly.

Ernestine said, "Watch it, Ray, or they'll shoot you, too."

When the cops could find no proof that Jimmy had been the spokesperson for simmering student revolt nor for the anti-poverty group that immediately endorsed his actions, they prepared to leave. Normally they lock a place back up, but since there didn't seem to be anything of value, they left me sitting on the edge of Jimmy's bed, barefoot and stupefied, the door swung open.

Now the huffer hauls Jimmy's codeine cough syrup out from behind the rusted can of Drain-o under the sink and it makes the rounds. A few good hits take me below seawater, to a new level of pre-consciousness. There's a deadening of the body, enhancement of certain senses, most notably hearing.

Darlene yaps again about the corpse, "Think he'll cree-mate? It costs, you know, you can't just dig a hole, someone's got to pay."

"Welfare," says Daryl.

"The daughter," says Mary Louise, "if there's no wife."

Me, I wonder.

And Darlene's mother nods vigorously. I can hear the flubbery shake of her goiterous neckskin. The creak of vinyl purse straps grasped tightly in her fingers. Polyester pant legs shimmering, pressed by hamhock thighs. The stretch of the nylon stitching that fights to keep those pants sewn together. A flesh orchestra—throat clearings, saliva swallowings, scalp scratchings, spine crackings. A soft gust of air being expelled from somebody's anus. Knees pop when someone's sorry weight heaves from one foot to the next.

I cannot move or speak.

Is this death?

After some bickering about his room—is it larger than the others, who has seniority and gets to switch—they leave, almost all at once. Even the dog skitters out after Daryl, who beats it back to three-oh-six, probably to snort a bump, and Jimmy's door swings open to sunset. Daylily and ripe tomato and burst peony.

"Don't go," I say, but no sound comes.

I remain prone.

I am gratified to survive the ritual. If this is survival.

I am one with Jimmy's berth.

Now I turn my mind to the beat of my heart: steady. The jumping skin at my wrist, my neck.

Once Jimmy and I were drinking at Penny's Open Mic and he stood in line to take his turn with the slam poets and folk-singers, the indie-rock douchebags. Jimmy had wolfgrowled and yodelled and shouted about tuberculosis, his childhood quarantine.

"Locked up with the freakshow! Ten years of suffering, suffering. Sanatorium released me to wander the streets, how kind! My family, *poof*, gone. Threw me in jail, said I disturbed the peace. I said, what peace? Ain't nothing peaceful left in this life!"

Poseurs clapped and bought him pints of draught. By way of thanks Jimmy said, "Got this plate in my head from the pig battering I took on the way downtown."

Poor old Jimmy.

A drink would be nice, whisky or bourbon. I'm not one for Scotch, Jimmy neither. Drinking and doping take me from misery, at first. Sooner or later they U-turn straight back to Delia or the times before—evictions, incarcerations, disinheritance—all my bantling failures, and often end in staggering tirades up and down Lansdowne Avenue while I try to purge myself of venom.

I'd shout, "Fuck you, Delia, fuck your greedy suck mouth!" Jimmy'd smoke a cigarette and wait for it to pass.

"Jimmy," I slurred on more than one occasion, my arm around his neck, "every time I touched that woman, she'd push away. Then complain I wasn't interested. She'd lie there, fuming. That woman gave me the limp dick. Used to like mowing the lawn; I couldn't get that right for her, either."

"Ray," Jimmy would say, "Biggie and I cannot abide coarse talk," and he'd shield his jacket pocket with a hand.

I'd say, "That woman was sent to test me, she was born to bring me down. Even my mother couldn't stand me. Even my father. I never finished anything, never had the chance to get it right!"

He'd said, "Bullshit, Ray. You made yourself into who you are. Now it's time to move on."

What kind of man says that? That's for fathers. For men of the cloth. Or a certain rare combination of the two.

When I picked fights, which was often, he'd step between me and the sonofabitch I'd provoked. He'd brace his hands on my shoulders and look me in the eye. He'd say, "You don't have to do this, son, you are better than this." Once my screaming subsided and my fists dropped, he'd say, "I got an itch to dance, Ray, let's smoke a bowl and listen to your government music box." My guess is that that man had single-handedly kept me out of jail the better part of three years. To think how I scored that H and tucked it away, wanting it all for myself—enough to feign illness to Jimmy's comprehending face and hole up for days, shooting it, dreaming it, filling my blackened soul with its magic—while out there, somewhere, Jimmy took his stand without me.

Twilight in Jimmy's bed: the blue hour, bruised plum bled to dusk. The grind of cars and trucks rounding the curve out on Lansdowne Avenue, honking, revving, squealing to brake at the light. Beeping: a city bus kneels to let widows and strollered mothers climb aboard. Planes pass overhead and their sonic rumble effects a loosening in my guts; it's a frequency I've heard all my life but never paid mind to. This vibration could be some sort of answer. When the Go Train counters with its relentless engines, its momentous reclamation of suited suburbanites, I feel the bedframe tremble and believe I might aneurism or perhaps orgasm with the drama. *Bee bop, diddily whop, bap bap, yeah!* These are sounds that bury a man, sounds a man can never climb back up and around, never in his miserable shit of a life. I spread my arms wide on Jimmy's cot.

Above me, Biggie Smalls spindles in the corner, lays her thousand cotton-swabbed eggs, sits the night in wait for prey. Later, later, the teeny tiny speckles shake themselves to life. They spin and descend the besmirched wall toward my cooling flesh. Creep their way to the dawn of a forgotten universe.

Acknowledgements

I'm extremely grateful to the Canada Council for the Arts, the Ontario Arts Council, and the Toronto Arts Council for financial support. Thank you to editors and staff at *Foglifter, FreeFall Magazine, Grain Magazine, Orca: A Literary Journal, The New Guard, The Tahoma Literary Review*, and *The Winnipeg Review*, who first published some of these stories.

For early draft insights, I thank Carolyn Beck, Anne Laurel Carter, Jani Krulc, Frances Key Phillips, Adam Prince, Shannon Quinn, Susan Safyan, Sarah Selecky, and Phoebe Tsang. Colossal thanks to Paige Cooper, Sister Valkyrie, for picking clean the bones. Sandra "Lady Monster" Kasturi for untold kindnesses, and Bink Dally Rue for surgical-tool sterilization procedures. Emily Donaldson, copy editrix extraordinaire. John Metcalf, tireless champion of the English language's extravagant potential. Dan Wells and the commendable Biblioasis team: thank you. Annetta and Patrick Dunnion and my siblings, for enduring support. Shannon Quinn, spirit animal; Helen Prancic, mistress of the dark web; John MacDonald, keeper of the home fires.